Jamaica Inn

DAPHNE DU MAURIER

Level 6

Retold by A S M Ronaldson
Series Editors: Andy Hopkins and Jocelyn Potter

Pearson Education Limited
Edinburgh Gate, Harlow,
Essex CM20 2JE, England
and Associated Companies throughout the world.

ISBN 0 582 41931X

First published in The Longman Simplified English Series 1962
This adaptation first published by Addison Wesley Longman Limited
in the Longman Fiction Series 1996
by arrangement with Victor Gollancz Ltd.
Third impression 1998
This edition first published 1999

Second impression 2000

This edition copyright © Penguin Books Ltd 1999
Cover design by Bender Richardson White

Set in 11/14pt Bembo
Printed in Spain by Mateu Cromo, S.A Pinto (Madrid)

Published by Pearson Education Limited in association with
Penguin Books Ltd, both companies being subsidiaries of Pearson Plc

For a complete list of the titles available in the Penguin Readers series please write to your local
Pearson Education office or to: Marketing Department, Penguin Longman Publishing,
5 Bentinck Street, London, W1M 5RN.

Contents

Introduction

"I was born on May 13th, 1907, into a world of make-believe and imagination," wrote Daphne du Maurier. Her father was Sir Gerald du Maurier, the leading actor and manager at Wyndham's Theatre in London. Her mother, Muriel, was an actress and her grandfather, George du Maurier, was an artist and writer. So Daphne and her two sisters grew up in an exciting world of writers and actors. She was educated at home, apart from six months spent in France when she was eighteen, and she read widely in English and French. Her first poems and short stories were written while she was still a child. "Books became my life ... from the start I was always pretending to be someone else in a story."

In 1926 Daphne travelled with her mother and sisters to Fowey in Cornwall, and this visit seems to have been an important turning point in her life. She fell in love with the place and its people, and was moved to write her first full-length work of fiction, *The Loving Spirit*. This romantic story was read by Frederick Browning, who was then a young officer in the Guards. It touched him so deeply that he travelled to Fowey in his boat to meet the person who had written it. In 1932 Browning and Daphne du Maurier were married. They had two daughters and a son. Du Maurier spent most of her adult life in the Cornwall which she loved so much and where her most popular books are set. She died there in 1989.

Du Maurier's books can be divided into two main groups. The first consists of historical fiction set in seventeenth- and eighteenth-century Cornwall; this includes *Jamaica Inn* (1936), *Frenchman's Creek* (1941), *Hungry Hill* (1943) and *The King's General* (1946). These are romantic stories of adventure, violence and love. They show a strong longing for the past, but also a sense

v

of how our present lives are affected by past events. The second group are modern mystery stories, including Rebecca (1938), My *Cousin Rachel* (1951) and *The Scapegoat* (1957). In addition, du Maurier wrote many books of short stories. Two short stories, 'The Birds' and 'Don't Look Now', were made into successful films of the same names. She also wrote non-fiction, including a book about her father's life, *Gerald: A Portrait* (1934), a family history, the story of her own life, books about Cornwall, and a study of Branwell Brontë.

The events in *Jamaica Inn* take place at the beginning of the nineteenth century. The setting is Bodmin Moor in Cornwall, a cold and lonely place in the south-west corner of Britain. The setting is very important as the dark events in the story could only take place in an area where there are few human beings to witness what is happening. Those that do live there are as cold and hard as their surroundings. When Mary arrives at the inn, she cannot help comparing the unwelcoming emptiness of the moor with the warmth of the village of Helford that she has just left.

The history of Cornwall is full of sea stories involving smugglers and wreckers. Smugglers often became romantic figures, more respected than the representatives of the law who were trying to catch them. Wreckers, on the other hand, were frightening figures who, as their name suggests, caused ships to be destroyed on the rocky coast. They shone lights out to sea from the rocks, which ships believed were the lights of the port. When the ships broke up, the wreckers stole the goods that floated to shore. But they didn't just steal; the wreckers always made sure that no one stayed alive to report what had happened.

The central character of this story, Mary Yellan, gains our sympathy by her courage in the face of evil. When we first meet her, she is an inexperienced girl who has lived in the same place for 23 years. She is alone after her mother's death, and appears a weak, defenceless figure. As the story develops, though, she fights back against the difficult situation she finds herself in and is not afraid to do what she believes to be right, even when this means putting her own life in danger. She is attracted by a certain amount of risk and danger, and falls in love with a man who seems to represent the possibility of both.

Mary Yellan is invited by her Aunt Patience to go and live with her and her husband, Joss Merlyn, after the death of Mary's mother. Joss is the landlord of Jamaica Inn, a mysterious place standing alone in the wild countryside of Bodmin Moor. Mary soon discovers that few guests come to stay at the inn, and respectable people avoid the place completely. Its landlord is an evil character who tries from the start to rule Mary's life as he does her aunt's. But Mary refuses to be frightened quite so easily, and is determined to uncover the secrets of the place. She badly needs friends, but who can she trust? Jem Merlyn, the landlord's attractive but horse-thieving brother? Or Francis Davey, the soft-spoken Vicar of Altarnun? As the situation becomes more and more dangerous for Mary, she has to decide where she can turn for help.

Chapter 1 Jamaica Inn

It was a cold grey day in late November, and although it was now only a little after two o'clock in the afternoon the dark of a winter eveninfg seemed to have come down over the hills, hiding them in mist. The air was cold, and in spite of the tightly closed windows it found its way into the coach. There must have been a small crack in the roof, because now and again little drops of rain fell softly through onto the leather seats. The wind blew hard, and on high ground it blew with such force that the whole body of the coach trembled and struggled to stay upright. The wheels of the coach sank into the holes in the road, and sometimes they threw up mud against the windows, where it mixed with the rain so that any view there might have been was blocked out.

The few passengers sat close together for warmth. Mary Yellan was sitting where the drops of rain came through the crack in the roof. She brushed them away with impatient fingers. Although she was only 40 miles by road from what had been her home for 23 years, she was already beginning to miss it. The courage which was so large a part of her, and had helped her so much during the long unhappiness of her mother's illness and death, was now shaken by this rain and wind.

She remembered the letter from her aunt. The writer said that the news had shocked her; that she had had no idea that her sister was ill, because it was many years since she had been in Helford. And she went on: 'There have been changes with us that you will not know about. I no longer live in Bodmin, but nearly 12 miles outside it, on the road to Launceston. It's a wild and lonely spot, and if you were to come to us I should be glad of your company in wintertime. I have asked your uncle, and he does not object, he says, if you do not talk too much and will give help when it is needed. He cannot give you money or feed you for nothing, as you will understand. He will expect your help in the bar in return for your room and meals. You see, your uncle is the landlord of Jamaica Inn.'

The letter was a strange message of welcome from the smiling Aunt Patience she remembered. A cold, empty letter, giving no word of comfort, and little information, except that she must not ask for money. Aunt Patience, with her silk skirts and delicate ways, the wife of an innkeeper!

So it was that Mary Yellan found herself travelling north in the coach. Villages were scattered now, and there were few smiling faces at the doors of the small houses. There were almost no trees. The wind blew and the rain came with the wind. And so the coach rolled into Bodmin, grey and unwelcoming like the hills around it, and one by one the passengers collected up their things ready to leave – all except Mary, who sat still in her corner. The driver, his face a stream of rain, looked in at the window.

'Are you going on to Launceston?' he said. 'It'll be a wild drive tonight across the moors. You can stay in Bodmin, you know, and go on by coach in the morning. There'll be no one but you going on in this coach.'

'My friends will be expecting me," said Mary. 'I'm not afraid of the drive. And I don't want to go as far as Launceston; will you please leave me at Jamaica Inn?'

The man looked at her strangely. 'Jamaica Inn?' he said. 'What would you do at Jamaica Inn? That's no place for a girl. You must have made a mistake, surely?' He looked at her hard, not believing her. Then he called over his shoulder to a woman who stood in the doorway of the Royal Hotel, lighting a lamp. It was already getting dark. 'Come here and reason with this young girl. I was told she was going to Launceston, but she has asked me to leave her at Jamaica Inn!'

The woman came down the steps and looked into the coach.

'It's a wild, rough place up there,' she said, 'and if you're looking for work, you won't find it on the farms. They don't like strangers on the moors. You'd do better down here in Bodmin.'

Mary smiled at her. 'I shall be all right,' she said. 'I'm going to relatives. My uncle is the landlord of Jamaica Inn.'

There was a long silence. In the grey light of the coach Mary could see that the woman and the man were looking at her. She felt cold, suddenly, and anxious. Then the woman stepped back from the window. 'I'm sorry,' she said. 'It's none of my business, of course. Good night.'

The driver began to whistle, rather red in the face, as one who wishes to end an awkward situation. Mary leant forward and touched his arm. 'Would you tell me?' she said. 'I shan't mind what you say. Is my uncle not liked? Is something the matter?'

The man looked very uncomfortable. He avoided her eyes. 'Jamaica Inn's got a bad name,' he said; 'strange stories are told – you know how it is. But I don't want to make any trouble. Perhaps they're not true.'

'What sort of stories?' asked Mary. 'Do you mean that people get drunk there? Does my uncle encourage bad company?'

The man did not answer. 'I don't want to make trouble,' he repeated, 'and I don't know anything. It's only what people say. Respectable people don't go to Jamaica Inn any more. That's all I know. In the old days we used to water the horses there, and feed them, and go in for a bite of food and drink. But we don't stop there any more.'

'Why don't people go there? What is their reason?'

The man paused; it was as if he were searching for words.

'They're afraid,' he said at last, and then he shook his head; he had no more to say. He shut the door and climbed into his seat.

The coach rolled away down the street, past the safe and solid houses, the busy lights, the scattered people hurrying home for supper, their figures bent against the weather. Now the horses were climbing the steep hill out of the town and, looking through the window at the back of the coach, Mary could see the lights of Bodmin fast disappearing, one by one, until the last was gone. She was alone now with the wind and the rain, and 12 long miles of empty moor between her and her journey's end. She sat in her corner, shaken from side to side by the coach. On either side of the road the countryside stretched away into space. No trees, no paths, no houses, but mile after mile of moor, dark and empty, rolling like a desert to the unseen horizon. No human being could live in this country, thought Mary, and remain like other people; the children would be born twisted, like the blackened bushes, bent by the force of a wind that never stopped blowing. Their minds would be twisted too, their thoughts evil, living as they must among rough bushes and hard stone.

She lifted the window and looked out. Ahead of her, at the top of hill on the left, was some sort of building, standing back from the road. She could see tall chimneys in the darkness. There was no other house near. If this was Jamaica Inn, it stood alone, unprotected from the winds. The horses came to a stop, clouds of steam rising from their hot, wet bodies.

The driver climbed down from his seat, pulling her box down with him. He seemed to be in a hurry, and kept looking over his shoulder towards the house.

'Here you are,' he said, 'across the yard over there. If you hammer on the door they'll let you in. I must be going on, or I'll not reach Launceston tonight.'

In a moment the coach was away down the road, disappearing as if it had never existed, lost and swallowed up in the darkness.

Mary stood alone, with her box at her feet. She heard the sound of the door being unlocked in the dark house behind her, and then it was thrown open. A great figure walked into the yard, swinging a light from side to side.

'Who is it?' came a shout. 'What do you want here?'

Mary stepped forward and looked up into the man's face. The light shone in her eyes, and she could see nothing.

'Oh, it's you, is it?' he said. 'So you've come to us after all? I'm your uncle, Joss Merlyn. Welcome to Jamaica Inn.' He pulled her into the shelter of the house, laughing, then shut the door and put the light on a table in the passage. And they looked at each other face to face.

Chapter 2   The Landlord

He was a great big man, nearly 7 feet high, with a lined face and dark brown skin. His thick black hair hung down over his eyes and round his ears. He looked as if he had the strength of a horse, with large, powerful shoulders, long arms that reached almost to his knees, and big hands. His nose was hooked, curving to a mouth that might have been perfect once but was now sunken and fallen, but there was still something fine about his great dark eyes, in spite of the lines around them. The best things left to him were his teeth, which were all good still, and very white, so that when he smiled they showed up clearly against the brown of his face; but it was a cold, evil smile.

'So you are Mary Yellan,' he said at last, towering above her, his head bent to examine her more closely, 'and you've come all this way to look after your Uncle Joss. I call it very nice of you.'

He laughed again, his laugh filling the house, and striking Mary, in her cold, tired anxiety, like a whip.

'Where is my Aunt Patience?' she asked, looking around her in the dark passage, with its cold stone floor and narrow staircase. 'Is she not expecting me, then?'

'Where's my Aunt Patience?' he repeated, copying the rise and fall of her voice. Then he lifted his face to the stairs.

'Patience!' he shouted, 'What are you doing? Here's the girl arrived, crying for you. She's tired of the sight of me already.'

There was a noise at the top of the stairs. Then down came a woman, her hand raised to keep the light from her eyes. She wore a cap on her thin grey hair, which hung to her shoulders. Her eyes were large, as though they were continually asking questions, and she had a little habit of moving her mouth – tightening her lips and then relaxing them. She wore an old striped skirt that had once been red and was now a pale pink. Mary watched her without speaking, full of sorrow. Was this poor creature the beautiful Aunt Patience of her dreams – dressed like this, and looking 20 years older than she was?

The little woman came down the stairs and into the hall; she took Mary's hands in hers and looked closely into her face. 'Have you really come?' she whispered. 'It *is* Mary Yellan, isn't it? My dead sister's child?'

Mary thanked God that her mother could not see her now. 'Dear Aunt Patience,' she said gently, 'I'm glad to see you again. It's so many long years since you came to us at Helford.'

The woman suddenly held her tightly, burying her head against her shoulder, and she began to cry, loudly and fearfully.

'Ah, stop that,' shouted the husband. 'What sort of welcome is this? What have you got to cry about, you fool? Can't you see the girl wants her supper? Get out to the kitchen and give her some meat and a drink.'

Aunt Patience controlled herself. She led the way to another dark passage, and so into the kitchen where a low fire burned.

'You mustn't mind your Uncle Joss,' she said, her manner changing suddenly to that of a dog that has been trained by continuous cruelty to unquestioning obedience and who, in spite of kicks and shouts, will fight like a tiger for his master. 'Your uncle must be treated carefully, you know; he has his ways, and strangers don't understand him at first. He's a very good husband to me, and has been ever since our wedding day.'

She talked on and on, going backwards and forwards across the stone-floored kitchen as she laid the table for supper. There was a footstep outside the door, and with a sinking heart Mary realized that Joss Merlyn had come downstairs again. He entered the room, and looked from one to the other. He pulled a chair from the wall, and crashed it against the table. Then he sat down heavily and, reaching for the loaf, cut himself a great piece of bread, which he pushed into his mouth, before calling Mary to the table. 'You need food, I can see that,' he said, and carefully buttered the loaf. He cut a thin piece from it and then cut this into four quarters for her, the whole business very delicately done and quite different from his manner in serving himself – so much so that to Mary there was something almost frightening in the change from roughness to gentle care. It was as if there was some power in his fingers which turned them suddenly and unexpectedly into skilful servants.

'Patience,' he said, 'here's the key. Go and get me a bottle, in the Lord's name – I've a terrible thirst!'

In a few minutes his wife returned with the alcohol, which she put in front of her husband, and while she finished her cooking and served Mary and herself, he began drinking, kicking the leg of the table. Suddenly he struck the table with his hand, shaking the plates and cups; one fell to the ground and broke.

'I'll tell you something, Mary Yellan,' he shouted, 'I'm master in this house, and I want you to know it. You'll do as you're told, and help in the house and serve in the bar, and I'll not lay a finger on you. But, by God, if you open your mouth, I'll punish you until you eat out of my hand the same as your aunt there.'

Mary faced him across the table. She held her hands below the table so that he could not see them tremble.

'I understand you,' she said. 'It doesn't matter to me what you do in the inn. I'll do my work in the house, and you'll have no cause to complain. But if you hurt my Aunt Patience in any way,

7

I tell you this – I'll leave Jamaica Inn immediately, and I'll find a magistrate and bring him here, and use the law against you; and then try to punish me if you like!'

Mary had turned very pale. She did not know it, but she had saved herself; her little show of courage had an effect on the man, who leant back in his chair and relaxed.

'That's very pretty,' he said; 'very prettily put. Now we know just what sort of visitor we have. Make her angry, and she shows her teeth. All right, my dear; you and I are more like each other than I thought. If we're going to play, we'll play together. I may have work for you at Jamaica Inn one day, work that you've never done before. Man's work, Mary Yellan, where you play with life and death.'

Mary heard a faint cry from Aunt Patience beside her. 'Oh, Joss,' she whispered. 'Oh, Joss, please!'

There was so much fear in her voice that Mary looked at her in surprise. Her uncle waved his hand impatiently.

'Get up to bed, Patience,' he said. 'I'm tired of your miserable face at my supper table. This girl and I understand each other.'

The woman rose immediately and went to the door. After a last helpless look over her shoulder, she went upstairs. Joss Merlyn and Mary were alone. He pushed the empty glass away from him and folded his arms on the table.

'There's been one weakness in my life, and I'll tell you what it is. It's drink. It's a curse, and I know it. I can't stop myself. One day it will be the end of me, and a good thing too. Days go by and I don't touch more than a drop. And then I'll feel the thirst come on me and I'll drink – drink for hours. I talk then – talk until everything I've done is told to the four winds. I've told you because I've already had too much and I can't hold my tongue. But I've not lost control of my head. I've not had enough to tell you why I live in this forgotten place, and why I'm the landlord of Jamaica Inn.' His voice was hardly more than a whisper. The fire had sunk low, and dark shadows stretched long fingers on the wall. The light on the table threw a great, ugly shadow of Joss Merlyn on the ceiling. 'The coaches don't stop here now. I don't worry; I've visitors enough. The farther the gentlemen keep away, the better pleased I am. Ah, there's drinking here all right, and plenty of it too. There are some who come to Jamaica Inn on Saturday night, and there are some who turn the key of their door and sleep with their fingers in their ears. There are nights when every house on the moors is dark and silent, and the only lights for miles are the windows of Jamaica Inn. They say the shouting and the singing can be heard as far down as the farms below Roughtor. You'll be in the bar those nights, if you like, and you'll see what company I keep.'

Mary sat very still, holding tightly to the sides of her chair.

'They're all afraid of me,' he went on; 'the whole cursed lot of them. Afraid of me, who's afraid of no man. It's the drink that's been against me. Drink and my hot blood. It's the curse of all of us, Mary. There's never been a Merlyn yet that died peaceful in his bed.

'My father was hanged at Exeter – he had a quarrel with a man, and killed him. I'm the oldest of three brothers, all born under the shadow of Kilmar. You walk out over there across the moor, and you'll see a great rock like a devil's hand sticking up into the sky. That's Kilmar. If you'd been born under its shadow you'd start to drink, as I did. My brother Matthew was drowned in Trewartha Marsh. We thought he'd gone to be a sailor, and had no news of him, and then in the summer no rain fell for seven months, and there was Matthew sticking up in the marsh, with his hands above his head, and the birds flying round him. My brother Jem was the baby. Hanging on to mother's skirts when Matthew and I were grown men. I never did agree with Jem. Too clever he is – too quick with his tongue. Oh, they will catch him in time and hang him, as they did my father.'

He was silent, looking into his empty glass. 'I've said enough. I'll have no more tonight. Go up to bed, Mary. You'll find your room above the front door.'

Mary was about to pass him when he seized hold of her shoulder and twisted her round.

'There'll be nights sometimes when you hear wheels on the road,' he said, 'and those wheels will not pass on, but they'll stop outside Jamaica Inn. And you'll hear footsteps in the yard, and voices beneath your window. When that happens, you'll stay in bed, Mary Yellan, and cover your head with the bedclothes. Do you understand?'

'Yes, uncle.'

'Very well. Now go, and if you ever ask me a question I'll break every bone in your body.'

She went out of the room, into the dark passage and up the stairs, feeling the wall with her hands. Her uncle had told her that her room was over the front door. Her box lay on the floor. The walls were rough and unpapered and the floorboards dirty. A box turned on its side served as a table, with a cracked mirror on top. The thin bedclothes were not dry enough to sleep under. She went to the window and looked out. The wind had gone down, but it was still raining – a thin, miserable rain that ran down the side of the house and mixed with the dirt on the window.

Whatever she would have to face in the future, and no matter how frightened she might be, she would not leave Jamaica Inn now. She must stay with Aunt Patience. She was needed here. And so Mary lay, fully dressed, on her hard bed, her mind working while she prayed for sleep. She counted the minutes and the hours of an endless night, and when the first bird sang in the field behind the house she counted no more, but slept like a dead thing.

Chapter 3   The Locked Door

Mary woke to a high wind from the west, and a thin watery sun.

After breakfast, during the usual morning housework, Mary was able to explore the inn more thoroughly. It was a dark place, with long passages and unexpected rooms. There was a separate entrance to the bar at the side of the house, and though the room was empty now, there was something heavy in the air from the last time it was full – a taste of old tobacco, the sour smell of drink and the suggestion of warm, unclean people crowded one against the other on the dark wooden seats. Down a passage in the opposite direction from the kitchen was another room, the door of which was locked. Mary went out into the yard to look at it through the window, but there was a board nailed up against the window frame, and she could not see inside. The house and other buildings formed three sides of the square that was the little yard. Beyond this lay the road, a thin white track that stretched to the horizon, surrounded on each side by the moors, brown and wet from the heavy rains. Mary went out on the road and looked round her, and as far as the eye could see there was nothing but the black hills and the moors. The grey stone inn, with its tall chimneys, was the only house in view.

She went back into the house to find Aunt Patience.

'Aunt Patience,' she began, 'why is my uncle the landlord of Jamaica Inn?' The sudden direct attack took the woman by surprise, and for a moment she looked back at Mary without reply. Then she went red. 'Well,' she said, 'it's – it's a very important place here, on the road. You can see that. This is the main road from the south. The coaches pass here twice a week. There are always travellers on the road. We do good trade here.'

'How can you say that, when the rooms are never used, and the bedrooms are fit only for rats and mice? I've seen them for myself.'

Her aunt was silent for a moment, working her mouth and twisting her fingers together. 'Your Uncle Joss doesn't encourage people to stay. We do a good trade, I've told you that. Men come in from the farms. There are farms and houses scattered all over the moors for miles around, and men come from there for a drink. There are evenings when the bar is full.'

'The driver of the coach yesterday said that respectable people did not come to Jamaica Inn any more. He said they were afraid.'

Aunt Patience changed colour. She was pale now, and her eyes moved from side to side. She swallowed, and ran her tongue over her lips.

'Your Uncle Joss has a quick temper,' she said; 'you have seen that for yourself. He is easily angered.'

Her eyes begged to be excused further questioning. Mary saw that she had suffered enough, but tried one more question.

'Aunt Patience,' she said, 'I want you to look at me and answer me this, and then I won't worry you again. What has the locked room at the end of the passage to do with the wheels that stop outside Jamaica Inn by night?'

As soon as she had spoken she was sorry. A strange expression came over the woman's face, and her great hollow eyes looked across the table in fear. Her mouth trembled, and one hand wandered to her throat.

Mary pushed back her chair and knelt by her side. She put her arms around Aunt Patience, and held her close, and kissed her hair.

'I'm sorry,' she said. 'Don't be angry with me. It's not my business, and I've no right to question you, and I'm ashamed of myself. Please, please forget what I said.'

Her aunt buried her face in her hands. Then she looked over her shoulder, as if she were afraid that Joss himself stood in the shadows behind the door.

'Things happen at Jamaica Inn, Mary, that I've never dared to breathe a word about. Bad things. Evil things. I can't ever tell you. I can't even admit them to myself. Some of it you'll come to know in time. You can't avoid it, living here. Your Uncle Joss mixes with strange men, who follow a strange trade. Sometimes they come by night, and from your window you will hear footsteps, and voices, and knocking at the door. Your uncle lets them in, and he takes them along the passage to that room with the locked door. Before day they are gone, and no sign is left that they have ever been. When they come, Mary, you will say nothing to me or to your Uncle Joss. You must lie in bed and put your hands over your ears.'

Then she rose from the table, and pushed her chair back, and Mary heard her climb the stairs with heavy feet.

◆

Joss Merlyn was away from the house for nearly a week, and during that time Mary learnt something about the area. After helping her aunt in the house and kitchen, she was free to wander where she pleased.

The moors were even wilder than she had at first supposed. Like a wide desert they rolled from east to west, with paths here and there across the surface, and great hills breaking the skyline. It was a silent, empty country, untouched by human hand; on the high tors the stones leant against one another in strange shapes, great watchmen who had stood there since the hand of God first formed them. Wild sheep lived on the high tors. Black cattle fed on the moors beneath, their careful feet choosing the firm ground, as with inborn knowledge they avoided the long, green grass that was not grass at all, but soft, dangerous marsh. There was a silence on the tors that belonged to another age; an age that is past and gone as though it had never been, an age when man did not exist.

One day Mary crossed the East Moor, in the direction that Joss had described to her on the first evening; and when she had gone some way and stood alone on a hill, surrounded on all sides by empty moors, she saw that the land sloped down to a deep and dangerous marsh, through which ran a stream. And rising beyond the marsh, away on the other side, pointing its fingers to the sky, was a great rock like a broken hand coming straight out of the moor, its surface neatly formed as if cut by an artist. So this was Kilmar Tor; and somewhere over there, where the hills hid the sun, Joss Merlyn had been born and his brother lived today. Below her in the marsh Matthew Merlyn had been drowned.

Mary turned her back on Kilmar and began to run across the moor; nor did she stop until the marsh disappeared below the level of the hill, and the tor itself was hidden. She had come farther than she had intended, and the way home was long. It seemed an age before the last hill was behind her, and the tall chimneys of Jamaica Inn stood out in front of her. As she crossed the yard, she noticed with a sinking heart that the stable door was open, and the horse was inside. Joss Merlyn had returned.

She opened the door as silently as possible, but it rubbed against the stone floor and made a noise in protest.

In a moment the landlord appeared and called to her as she started up the stairs to her room.

'Here,' he said, 'no hiding up there this evening. There will be work for you in the bar, with your uncle. Don't you know what day of the week it is?'

Mary paused to think. She was losing count of time. Was it Monday's coach she had taken? That made today Saturday – Saturday night. Immediately she realized what Joss Merlyn meant. Tonight there would be company at Jamaica Inn.

Chapter 4   Wagons in the Night

They came one by one, the people of the moors, crossing the yard quickly and silently, as if they had no wish to be seen. They were a strange collection grouped around Joss Merlyn in the bar. Half hidden by rows of bottles and glasses, Mary could look down on the company and remain unseen. They lay on the seats; they leant against the walls; they sat beside the tables; and one or two, whose heads or stomachs were weaker than the rest, already lay full length on the floor. Most of them were dirty, with long hair and broken fingernails: cattle-stealers, sailors, wandering salesmen, thieves. The smell of drink and tobacco and unwashed bodies was strong. Mary felt disgust rise up in her, and she knew that she would give way to it if she stayed there long. The evening seemed endless, and her one thought was of escape. The air was so thick with smoke and breath that it was hard to see across the room, and to her tired, half-closed eyes the faces of the men seemed shapeless, all hair and teeth, their mouths much too large for their bodies, while those who had drunk too much lay on the seats or on the floor like dead men, their faces in their hands.

Those who could still stand had crowded round a dirty little pedlar from Redruth, who had made himself the joker of the group. The mine where he had worked was now in ruins, and he had taken to the road as a pedlar, and had stored up a collection of songs with which he now entertained the company. The laughter that greeted his rude songs and jokes nearly shook the roof. To Mary there was something horrible in this ugly, shouting laughter, which in some strange way held no note of amusement, but rang down the dark stone passages and into the empty rooms above, filling them with hopelessness. Mary could bear it no longer. She touched her uncle on the shoulder, and he turned to her, his face red with the heat of the room.

'I can't stand this,' she said. 'You'll have to serve your friends yourself. I'm going upstairs to my room.'

'Had enough of it, have you? Think yourself too good for us? Get out, then; it's nearly midnight, in any case, and I don't want you. You'll lock your door tonight, Mary. Your aunt's been in bed for an hour with the bedclothes over her head.'

He lowered his voice; bending down to her ear and seizing her wrist, he twisted it behind her back until she cried out in pain.

'Keep your mouth shut and I'll treat you gently. It is unwise to put your nose in where it is not wanted at Jamaica Inn, and you'd better remember that.'

Mary ran out of the room, shutting the door hard behind her, and as she went up the stairs, her hands over her ears, she could not keep out that sound of laughter and wild singing that sounded down the empty passage, following her to her room and even coming up through the cracks between the floorboards. Then she did as her uncle had told her. She undressed hurriedly and crept into bed, pulling the bedclothes over her head and putting her fingers in her ears, her only thought now to shut out the noise below.

She slept. Then, without warning, she was suddenly awake, sitting up in bed. She listened, hearing nothing at first except the beating of her own heart, but in a few minutes there came another sound, from beneath her room this time – the sound of heavy objects being dragged along the stone floor in the passage downstairs.

She got out of bed and went to the window, opening the shutters a crack. By the light of the moon she could see five wagons in the yard outside. Three were covered, each pulled by a pair of horses, and the remaining two were not. One of the covered wagons stood directly beneath the window, and the horses were steaming. Around the wagons were some of the men who had been drinking in the bar earlier in the evening. And there were strangers in the yard whom Mary had never seen before. She watched and began to understand. Packages and boxes were brought by the wagons and unloaded at Jamaica Inn. They were now being stored in the locked room. Everything was done in complete silence; the men who had shouted and sung earlier that night were now quiet and serious, their thoughts on nothing but the job.

Joss Merlyn came out of the front door, the pedlar at his side.

'Is that everything?' he called softly, and the driver of the last wagon waved and held up his hand. So the wagons moved away from Jamaica Inn, moving out of the yard one after another, some turning north and some south when they came out on to the road, until they had all gone, and there was no one left standing in the yard but one man whom Mary had not seen before, the pedlar, and the landlord of Jamaica Inn himself. Then they, too, turned and went back into the house. She heard them go along the passage in the direction of the bar, and then a door closed. There was no other sound except that of the big clock in the hall, which rang the hour – three o'clock.

Mary came away from the window and sat down on the bed. The cold air blew in onto her shoulders, and she trembled. This was smuggling on a grand scale. Had Joss Merlyn the necessary brain and skills to lead such a business? Had he been making preparations for tonight's work during the past week, when he was away from home? The men working for him must be carefully picked, in spite of their wild appearance, and the whole business carefully controlled, or they could never have escaped the law for so long. A magistrate who suspected smuggling would surely have suspected the inn unless he were involved himself. If it were not for Aunt Patience she would walk out of the inn now, find her way to the nearest town and give information about Joss Merlyn. He would soon be in prison, and the rest of them with him, and there would be an end to the trade.

But had she seen only part of the business, and was there still

17

more for her to learn? She remembered the fear in Aunt Patience's eyes, and those words spoken when the shadows crept across the kitchen floor: 'There are things happen at Jamaica Inn, Mary, that I've never dared to breathe a word about. Bad things. Evil things. I can't ever tell you. I can't even admit them to myself.' And she had climbed the stairs to her room, dragging her feet as she went, like an old woman. Smuggling was dangerous; it was dishonest; it was strictly forbidden by the law of the land; but was it evil? Mary needed advice, and there was no one she could ask. Here she was, a girl of twenty-three, with no weapons except her own brain to fight a man twice her size and eight times her strength.

'I'll not show fear before Joss Merlyn or any man,' she said. 'I will go down now and take a look at them in the bar, and if they kill me it will be my own fault.'

She dressed hurriedly, and then, opening her bedroom door, she stood and listened for a moment, hearing nothing but the sound of the clock in the hall. She crept out into the passage, and came to the stairs. By now she knew that the third step from the top would make a noise, and so would the last. She stepped gently, and so she came to the dark hall by the front door, empty except for one unsteady chair and the great clock.

As she paused, a sudden beam of light shone into the passage, and she heard voices. The door of the bar had swung open. The men must be sitting in silence on the seats against the outside wall, because she could not see or hear them. Then suddenly a voice rang out, high and trembling, the voice of a stranger.

'No, and no again. I tell you for the last time, I'll have no part in it. I'll break with you now, and for ever, and put an end to the agreement. That's murder you want me to do, Mr Merlyn; there's no other name for it — it's common murder.'

Someone — the landlord himself, no doubt — answered in a low voice. Mary could not catch his words, but his speech was

18

broken by a burst of laughter that she recognized as belonging to the pedlar.

He must have asked a question because the stranger's voice was heard again. 'Hanging, is it? I've risked hanging before, and I'm not afraid for my neck. No, I'm thinking of my soul and of God above. When it comes to the killing of harmless people, and perhaps women and children among them, that's evil, Joss Merlyn, and you know it as well as I do.'

Mary heard the sound of a chair being pulled back, and the man rising to his feet; then her uncle raised his voice for the first time.

'Not so fast, my friend,' he said, 'not so fast! You're in this business as far as you can be. I tell you there's no going back now; it's too late; too late for you and for all of us. I've been doubtful of you from the first, with your gentleman's ways and your clean shirts, and by God I've proved myself right. Harry, lock the door over there and put the bar across it.'

There was a sudden cry, and the sound of someone falling, and at the same time the table crashed to the floor. Once more the pedlar laughed his disgusting laugh, and he began to whistle one of his songs.

'Harry, stand where you are by the door, and put your knife in him if he tries to pass you. Now, look here, Mr Lawyer-clerk, or whatever you are, you've made a fool of yourself tonight, but you're not going to make a fool of me. You'd like to walk out of that door, wouldn't you, and get on your horse, and ride away to Bodmin? Yes, and by nine in the morning you'd have every magistrate in the country at Jamaica Inn, and a group of soldiers too. That's your fine idea, isn't it?'

Mary could hear the stranger breathing heavily, and he must have been hurt; for when his voice came it was sharp but faint. 'Do your devil's work if you must. I can't stop you, and I give you my word that I'll not give information about you. But join you I will not, and there's my last word to you both.'

There was a silence, and then Joss Merlyn spoke again. 'Take care,' he said softly. 'I heard another man say that once, and five minutes later he was walking in air. On the end of a rope it was, my friend, and his big toe just missed the floor. I asked him if he liked to be so near the ground, but he didn't answer. The rope forced the tongue out of his mouth, and he bit it in two. They said afterwards that he had taken seven and three-quarter minutes to die.'

Outside in the passage, Mary felt herself go cold and her arms and legs were suddenly as heavy as lead. With a growing sense of fear she realized that she was probably going to faint.

Her uncle's voice came from very far away. 'Leave me alone with him, Harry,' he said. 'There'll be no more work for you tonight at Jamaica Inn. Take his horse and go. I'll settle this business by myself.'

Somehow Mary found her way back down the passage and, hardly knowing what she was doing, she turned the handle of a door in the hall and fell inside.

She must have fainted and been unconscious for a minute or two, before she sat up again. She heard the sound of a horse in the yard outside, Harry the pedlar riding away, and then a sound from above made her lift her head. A floorboard once, and then again: quiet footsteps above. Mary's heart began to beat faster, and her breath came quickly. Whoever was hiding up above must have been there for hours. He must have hidden so that he would remain unseen by the smugglers. Someone – a friend perhaps – was hiding in the room next to her bedroom, and could help her to save the stranger in the bar.

But as she waited, trembling, she heard the landlord pass across the hall and climb the stairs. His footsteps stopped above her head. Then he knocked, very softly, on the door. Once more the floorboard made a noise as someone crossed the floor, and the door was opened from inside. Mary's heart sank, and her misery returned. Her uncle had known him to be there all the time, and that was why he had sent the pedlar away. He did not wish the pedlar to see his friend. Now they were coming down the stairs; they stopped for a moment outside the door of the room that Mary had entered, and for a moment she thought that they were coming inside. They were so close to her that she could have touched her uncle on the shoulder through the crack of the door. Then he spoke, and his voice whispered right against her ear.

'You must say. It's your judgment now, not mine. I'll do it, or we'll do it between us. It's you who must say the word.'

Hidden as she was by the door, Mary could neither see nor hear her uncle's new companion, and whatever sign he made in reply escaped her. They did not stay outside the room, but went off along the passage to the bar. Then the door closed, and she heard them no more.

Her first desire was to run out into the road, and so away from them, but she soon realized that by doing that she would gain nothing; quite possibly there might be other men on guard along the high road. She must have stood for ten minutes or more waiting for some sound or signal, but everything was still. Only the clock in the hall made its usual noises, unaffected by events. Then she went out into the dark passage. No crack of light came out under the door to the bar. She laid her ear against it. There was no sound. Through the keyhole came a steady current of cold air. Mary thought for a moment; then she opened the door and stepped into the room.

There was nobody there. The door leading to the yard was open, and the room was filled with fresh November air. The seats were empty, and the table that had crashed to the ground still lay on the floor, its legs pointing to the ceiling.

A last little beam of moonlight made a white circle on the

floor, and into the circle moved a dark shape like a finger. It was a shadow. Mary looked up to the ceiling and saw that a rope had been thrown over a hook in a beam. It was the rope's end that made the shadow in the circle; and it kept moving backwards and forwards, blown by the wind from the open door.

Chapter 5   Jem Merlyn

As the days passed, Mary Yellan settled down to life at Jamaica Inn with a sense of determination. It was clear that she could not leave her aunt to face the winter alone; she must make the best of the six months that lay ahead. If possible, she was determined to defeat her uncle and deliver him and his companions to the law. The events of that first Saturday night were never far from her mind, and the meaning of the rope's end hanging from the beam was clear. Mary had no doubt that the stranger had been killed by her uncle and another man, and his body buried somewhere on the moors. There was nothing to prove it, though, and in the light of day the story seemed unlikely.

Two weeks went by, and there was no Saturday night like the first one. No one came to the inn. The future seemed very black at times, especially as Aunt Patience made little effort to be a close companion; and though now and again she took hold of Mary's hand, telling her how glad she was to have her in the house, most of the time the poor woman existed in a dream, going about her duties without thinking and rarely speaking.

One morning Mary decided to clean down the long stone passage that ran the full width of the back of the house. As she was doing this, she heard the sound of a horse in the yard, and a moment later someone thundered on the closed door of the bar.

No one had come near Jamaica Inn before, and this knock on the door was an unusual event. Mary wiped her hands and went into the bar. A man was sitting there, with a glass in his hand which he had calmly filled for himself. For a few minutes they considered each other in silence. Something about him was familiar, and Mary wondered where she had seen him before. The heavy eyes, the curve of his mouth, and the shape of his jaw, even the look which he gave her, were known to her and disliked. The sight of him examining her and drinking at the same time made her angry.

'What do you think you're doing?' she said. 'You haven't any right to walk in here and help yourself.'

The man finished his drink, and held out his glass to be refilled.

'Since when have they kept a bar girl at Jamaica Inn?' he asked her, and, feeling in his pocket for a pipe, he lit it, blowing a great cloud of smoke in her face. His manner angered Mary even more, and she leant forward and pulled the pipe out of his hand, throwing it behind her onto the floor, where it broke.

'Is this how they train you to serve your customers? I don't think much of their choice. Fill up my glass! That's what you're here for, isn't it?' he said.

'As you seem to know your way about here, you can fill your own glass. I'll tell Mr Merlyn you are in the bar, and he can serve you himself if he likes.'

'Oh, don't worry Joss. What's happened to his wife? Has he sent her away to make room for you? I call that unkind to the poor woman!'

'Do you want to speak to the landlord or not? I can't stand here all day. If you don't want to see him, and you have finished your drink, you can put your money on the table and leave.'

The man laughed. 'Do you give orders to Joss in that way?' he said. 'He must be a changed man if you do.'

'Joss Merlyn is my uncle by marriage,' she said. 'My name is Mary Yellan, if that means anything to you. There's the door behind you. Good morning.'

She left the bar, meeting the landlord himself in the doorway.

'Oh, it's you, Jem, is it? What do you want at Jamaica Inn?' He closed the door behind him, leaving Mary in the passage outside.

She went back to her bucket of water. So that was Jem Merlyn, her uncle's younger brother. Of course – he had reminded her of her uncle all through the conversation, though she had not realized it. He had Joss Merlyn's eyes, without the lines round them, and he had Joss Merlyn's mouth – firm, though, where the landlord's was weak. He was what Joss Merlyn might have been 18 or 20 years ago, but smaller and neater. This Jem had the same cruelty in him as his brother – she could see it in the shape of his mouth. Aunt Patience had said he was the worst of the family.

She was so busy that she did not hear the stones thrown at the window of the room, and it was not until one cracked the glass that, looking out of the window, she saw Jem Merlyn standing in the yard beside his horse.

Mary unlocked the heavy entrance door and went out.

'What do you want now?' she asked him.

'Forgive me if I was rude to you just now,' he said. 'Somehow I didn't expect to see a woman at Jamaica Inn – well, not a young girl like you. I know I deserve black looks for behaving as I did, but if you knew my brother as well as I do you'd understand how I made the mistake. It looks strange, having a girl at Jamaica Inn. Why did you come here in the first place?'

He looked serious now, and his likeness to Joss had gone for the moment. She wished he were not a Merlyn.

'I came here to be with my Aunt Patience,' she said. 'My mother died some weeks ago, and I have no other relative. I'll tell you one thing, Mr Merlyn – I am thankful my mother isn't alive to see her sister now.'

'You haven't a good opinion of the landlord, then?'

24

'No, I have not,' she replied. 'He's turned my aunt from a laughing, happy woman into a miserable slave, and I'll never forgive him for that as long as I live.'

'We Merlyns have never been good to our women. I can remember my father beating my mother until she couldn't stand. She never left him, though. When he was hanged at Exeter she never spoke a word for three months. Her hair went white with the shock. What she found to love in him, I can't say – he never asked for her after he'd been taken, and he left all his money to another woman on the other side of the river.'

Mary was silent. The lack of feeling in his voice shocked her. He spoke without shame or sorrow, and she supposed that he had been born, like the rest of his family, without any warmth or gentleness.

'How long do you mean to stay at Jamaica Inn?' he asked suddenly. 'There's not much company for you here.'

'I'm not going away unless I take my aunt with me. I'd never leave her alone, after what I have seen.'

'What have you learnt, in your short time? It's quiet enough here.'

Mary thought that he might be trying to make her talk. It was possible that her uncle had suggested that his brother should speak to her, hoping in this way to obtain information.

'I helped my uncle in the bar one Saturday night, and I didn't care for the company he kept.'

'I don't suppose you did. The men who come to Jamaica Inn have never been taught manners. They spend too much time in prison.'

'What do you do for a living?' asked Mary with sudden interest, for he spoke better than his brother.

'I'm a horse thief,' he said cheerfully, 'but there's not much money in it, really. My pockets are always empty.'

'Aren't you afraid of being caught?' said Mary.

'Stealing is an awkward thing to prove. Suppose a horse wanders away and his owner goes to look for him. These moors are full of wild horses and cattle. It's not going to be easy to find his horse. Say the horse had long hair, and one white foot, and a diamond mark in his ear. Off goes the owner to Launceston market with his eyes wide open. But he doesn't find his horse. It's there, of course, but its hair is cut short, its four feet are all the same colour, and the mark in its ear is a square not a diamond. The owner doesn't look at it twice. That's simple enough, isn't it?'

Mary laughed, in spite of herself. He was so open in his dishonesty that she could not be angry with him.

Jem Merlyn looked at her seriously, and then he bent towards her, first looking quickly over her head into the door beyond.

'Look here,' he said, 'I'm serious now; you can forget all the nonsense I've told you. Jamaica Inn is no place for a girl – nor for any woman, if it comes to that. Why don't you run away? I could put you on the road to Bodmin.'

Mary could almost have trusted him. But she could not forget that he was Joss Merlyn's brother, and, being that, might deceive her. Time would show whose side he was on.

'I don't need any help,' she said. 'I can look after myself.'

Jem threw his leg over his horse's back. 'All right,' he said. 'I won't worry you. My house is the other side of Trewartha Marsh. I shall be there until the spring, at least. Good day to you.' And he was off, and away down the road before she had time to say a word in reply.

Mary went slowly back into the house, and the cold, dead air of Jamaica Inn closed round her again.

Chapter 6   Mr Bassat's Visit

That night the wagons came again. This time they arrived empty, and were loaded with the last of the goods which had been left at the inn the time before. Mary guessed that this was their way of working. The inn was used as a store for a few weeks at a time and then, when the opportunity came, the wagons set out once more, and the goods were carried to the river bank and transported to different places from there. The organization must be a big one, and there would be agents scattered far and wide who kept the necessary watch on events. It was with a sudden sting of disappointment that Mary wondered whether the visit of Jem Merlyn to Jamaica Inn that morning had been important. How strange that the wagons came so soon after him! He had come from Launceston, he said, and Launceston stood on the river bank. Mary was angry with him and with herself. In spite of everything, her last thought before sleeping had been the possibility of his friendship. She would be a fool if she had hopes of it now. Jem might disagree with his brother, but it was clear that they were both in the same trade. It was a miserable, bad business in every way, and here she was in the middle of it all, with Aunt Patience like a child to be looked after.

The next few days passed uneventfully. Then there came a fine cold morning when, for a change, the sun shone in a cloudless sky. Mary, whose spirits always rose at the sight of the sun, had turned her morning into a washing day; she felt well, and sang as she worked. Her uncle had ridden away on the moors somewhere, and a sense of freedom possessed her whenever he was away.

An urgent knocking at the window made her look up, and she saw Aunt Patience making signs to her, very white in the face and clearly frightened. Mary wiped her hands and ran to the back door of the house.

27

'It's Mr Bassat from North Hill,' Aunt Patience whispered. 'I saw him from the window. He's come on horseback, and another gentleman with him. Oh, my dear, my dear, what are we going to do?'

Mary thought quickly. She was in a very difficult position. If this Mr Bassat represented the law, it was her one chance of telling someone about her uncle. She could tell him about the wagons and about everything that she had seen since her arrival. She looked down at the trembling woman at her side. By now there was a continuous hammering on the door.

'Mary, if Mr Bassat asks you what you know, you won't answer him, will you? I can trust you, can't I? You'll not tell him of the wagons? If any danger came to Joss I'd kill myself, Mary.'

There was no argument after that.

Mary opened the heavy entrance door. There were two men outside. One had climbed down from his horse; it was he who had rained the blows on the door. The other was still on horseback. His face was brown and heavily lined; Mary judged him to be about fifty years of age.

'You don't hurry here, do you?' he called. 'There doesn't seem to be much of a welcome for travellers. Is the landlord at home?'

'If you please, Mr Bassat, my husband went out as soon as he had eaten his breakfast, and whether he will be back before night I cannot say.'

'That's a pity. I wanted a word or two with Mr Joss Merlyn.' Mr Bassat climbed heavily to the ground. 'While I'm here I may as well look round, and I'll tell you here and now it's useless to refuse me. I am a magistrate, and I have the necessary documents.' He pushed his way past the two women. Aunt Patience made a movement as though to prevent him, but Mary said quietly. 'Let him go. If we try to stop him now we shall only anger him the more.'

The rooms were thoroughly explored. The magistrate looked

into the dusty corners, lifted old bags and boxes, examined the stores of food, all the time crying out in anger and disgust. 'Call this an inn, do you? You haven't even got a bed fit for a cat to sleep on. The place is horrible. What does it mean, eh? Have you lost your tongue, Mrs Merlyn?'

The poor woman could not reply; she kept shaking her head and working her mouth, and Mary knew that she was wondering what would happen when they came to the locked room in the passage.

'What about you, young woman? Have you anything to say?'

'I'm here to look after my aunt. She's not very strong; you can see that for yourself. She's easily frightened.'

'I don't blame her, living in a place like this. Well, kindly show me the room that has barred windows. I noticed it from the yard, and I'd like to see inside.'

'I'm very sorry, sir,' Mary replied, 'but if you mean the old store room at the end of the passage, I'm afraid the door is locked. My uncle always keeps the key, and where he puts it I don't know.'

'Well, that's easily settled. We'll have the door down in no time.' He went out into the yard to call his servant. In a few minutes he returned with his man, Richards, who was carrying an iron bar which he had found in the stable. For a few minutes the door bore every blow. Then there was a splitting of wood and a crash, and the door gave way. It was dark of course; the blocked windows kept the light out. The servant produced a light, and the magistrate stepped into the room.

For a moment there was silence as the magistrate turned, letting the light shine in every corner, and then, making sounds of annoyance and disappointment, he faced the little group behind him.

'Nothing,' he said; 'nothing at all. The landlord has made a fool of me again.'

Except for a pile of empty bags in one corner, there was nothing in the room. It was thick with dust. There was no furniture of any sort, the fireplace had been blocked up with stones and the floor itself was of stone like the passage outside. On top of the bags lay a length of twisted rope.

Then the magistrate turned once more into the passage.

'Well, Mr Joss Merlyn has won this time. I'll admit myself beaten. Now listen to me,' he said, pointing his whip at Mary. 'This aunt of yours may have lost her tongue, but you can understand plain English, I hope. Do you mean to tell me you know nothing of your uncle's business? Does nobody ever call here, by day or night?'

Mary looked him straight in the eye. 'I've never seen anyone,' she said.

'Have you ever looked into that locked room before today?'

'No.'

'Have you any idea why he should keep it locked up?'

'No, none at all.'

'Have you ever heard wheels in the yard by night?'

'I'm a very heavy sleeper. Nothing ever wakes me.'

'Where does your uncle go when he's away from home?'

'I don't know.'

'Don't you think it's very strange, to keep an inn on the main road and then to close your door to every traveller?'

'My uncle is a very strange man.'

'That is true. In fact, he's so strange that half the people in the countryside won't sleep quietly in their beds until he's been hanged, like his father before him. You can tell him that from me.' He climbed onto his horse. 'One other thing,' he called. 'Have you seen anything of your uncle's younger brother, Jem Merlyn, of Trewartha?'

'No,' said Mary steadily. 'He never comes here.'

'Oh, doesn't he? Well, that's all I want from you this morning.

Good day to you both.' And away the two men went from the yard, and so on to the road.

Joss Merlyn returned just before midday. Mary told him calmly what had happened during the morning. He swore and shouted, but he was frightened, she could see that, and his confidence was shaken.

'Get me something to eat,' he said. 'I must go out again, and there's no time to waste. You've done well today, Mary, and I'll not forget it.'

She looked him in the eyes. 'You don't think I did it for you, do you?'

'I don't care why you did it; the result's the same.'

As soon as he had finished his meal, the landlord rose to his feet and left the kitchen. Mary watched him cross the moor. She thought for a moment, doubting the wisdom of the sudden plan in her head, and then she ran down the field after her uncle. When she reached the bottom, she bent down beside the stone wall until his figure crossed the skyline and disappeared, and then she jumped up again and followed him, picking her way across the rough grass and stones. It was crazy, no doubt, but her idea was to keep Joss Merlyn in view, and in this way to learn something of his secret plan. After a few miles she realized how difficult it was. She had to keep a good distance between them in order to remain unseen, and the landlord walked at such a speed that before long she saw that she would be left behind. The ground was now soft beneath her feet; the whole of the low-lying plain ahead of her was wet with winter rains. Her uncle had crossed the worst of the low ground with the quickness given by many years of practice. Then he was hidden by a big rock and she saw him no more.

It was impossible to discover the path which he had taken across the marsh, but Mary followed as best she could. She was a fool to attempt it, she knew, but a sort of determined stupidity

31

made her continue. When she reached the top of the hill, the evening clouds were thick and the world was grey. The horizon was hidden. Mary would never find her uncle now. She knew herself to be a fool for having gone so far on a December afternoon; experience had proved to her that when darkness came on Bodmin moor it was sudden and without warning. The low cloud over the marshes was dangerous too. But there was less danger from the marshes if she kept to the high ground, so, pulling up her skirt, she walked steadily forward, feeling the ground with some care when in doubt, and avoiding those places where the grass felt soft and gave way under her feet. Her legs were heavy, and her feet felt as if they hardly belonged to her, and her eyes felt sunken away back in her head. She walked on, her head low and her hands at her side, thinking that the tall grey chimneys of Jamaica Inn would be, for the first time, a welcome sight. The path was wider now, and was crossed by another running from left to right, and Mary stood uncertainly for a few moments, wondering which to take. It was then that she heard the sound of a horse coming out of the darkness to the left.

Mary waited in the middle of the track, and after some time the horse appeared out of the low cloud in front of her. The horseman turned sharply to the side as he saw Mary, and stopped.

'Hello,' he cried, 'who's there? Is anyone in trouble?' Then, looking down closely, he said in surprise, 'A woman! What in the world are you doing out here?'

'Can you help me to find the road? I'm miles from home and hopelessly lost.'

'Steady there!' he said to his horse. 'Stand still, will you? Where have you come from? Of course I will help you if I can.' His voice was low and gentle.

'I live at Jamaica Inn,' she said, and as soon as the words were out of her mouth she wished she had not said them. For a moment the man was silent, but when he spoke again his voice had not changed, but was quiet and gentle as before.

'Jamaica Inn?' he said. 'You've come a long way in the wrong direction, I'm afraid. You're tired out. You're not fit to walk another step; and what's more, I'm not going to let you. We're not far from the village, and you shall ride there. You shall come home with me, and dry your clothes and rest a little and have some supper before I take you back myself to Jamaica Inn.' He spoke with such kindness, but with such firmness, that Mary trusted him. Then she saw his eyes for the first time beneath the edge of his hat. They were strange eyes, like glass, and so pale in colour that they seemed near to white. His hair was white, too, under his black hat, and Mary looked at him in some surprise, because his face was unlined and his voice was not that of an old man.

Then, with sudden embarrassment, she understood, and she turned away her eyes. He was an albino.

He took off his hat. 'Perhaps I had better introduce myself,' he said with a smile. 'Even if the meeting is unusual, it is the right thing to do I believe. My name is Francis Davey, and I am the Vicar of Altarnun.'

Chapter 7   The Vicar of Altarnun

There was something strangely peaceful about his house. Mary stretched out her hands towards the fire. The silence pleased her; it took away her fear. She watched Francis Davey as he laid the table for supper. 'Hannah lives in the village,' he said. 'She leaves every afternoon at four. I prefer to be by myself. I like getting my own supper, and then I can choose my own time.'

She had not yet become used to his white hair and his eyes; his black clothes made them even more noticeable. She was tired, but she swallowed her supper. He poured her out a steaming cup of tea. Now and again she took a quick look at him, but he seemed to sense it immediately, for he would turn his eyes on her with their cold white look – like that of a blind man – and she would look away again. The warmth of the room and the hot tea made her sleepy, and his gentle voice came from far away.

'Why were you wandering on the moor tonight?'

Hardly knowing how it happened, she heard her voice reply to his.

'I'm in terrible trouble,' she said. 'Sometimes I think I shall become like my aunt, and go out of my mind. I've not been at Jamaica Inn much more than a month, but it seems like 20 years. It's my aunt that worries me; if only I could take her away! But she won't leave Uncle Joss, in spite of his treatment of her. Every night when I go to bed I wonder if I shall wake up and hear the wagons. The first time they came, there were six or seven of them, and they brought great packages and boxes that the men stored in the locked room at the end of the passage. A man was killed that night; I saw the rope hanging from a beam downstairs.' She stopped, the warm colour flooding her face. 'I've never told anyone before. It had to come out. I couldn't keep it to myself any longer. I've done something terrible.' For a moment or two he did not answer; then he spoke gently and slowly.

'Don't be afraid. Your secret is safe; no one shall know of this but me. When you have rested, I'll take you back, and I'll make your excuses to the landlord if you wish.'

'Oh, you mustn't do that,' said Mary quickly. 'If he suspects half of what I've done tonight he would kill me, and you too. You don't understand. He's a violent man, and nothing would stop him.'

'Isn't your imagination running away with you a little?' said the vicar. 'This is the nineteenth century, you know, and men don't murder one another without reason. Having gone so far, don't you think you had better let me hear the rest of your story?

What is your name, and why are you living at Jamaica Inn?'

Mary looked up at the pale eyes in the colourless face, at his white hair, and she thought again how strange he was, this man who might be twenty-one, who might be sixty, and who with his soft voice could persuade her to admit every secret she possessed if he wanted. She could trust him; that, at least, was certain.

The first part of her story was told in short and broken sentences, beginning with that first Saturday night at the bar, and then working backwards to her arrival at the inn. Her report did not sound true, even to her who knew the truth of it, and she was so tired that she often could not find the words, but paused for thought and then went back in her story and repeated herself. He heard her to the end with patience, but all the time she felt his eyes watching her, and he had a habit of swallowing from time to time which she came to recognize, and wait for.

When she had finished, the vicar got up from his chair and began to walk around the room.

'I believe you, of course,' he said, after a moment or so, 'but your story wouldn't be believed in a court of law. And another thing – it's wrong, we all know that, but smuggling goes on all over the country, and half the magistrates make a profit out of it. That shocks you, doesn't it? But you can be sure that it's the truth. I have met Mr Bassat once or twice, and I believe him to be an honest sort of man, but, between ourselves, a bit of a fool. I can tell you one thing, though; his visit will have frightened your uncle. There won't be any more wagons to Jamaica Inn for some time; I think you can be certain of that. If I were you, I should just wait. Keep a close watch on your uncle, and when the wagons do come again you can tell me immediately. We can then decide together what should be done.'

'What about the stranger who disappeared? He was murdered, I'm certain of that. Do you mean to say that nothing can ever be done about it?'

'I'm afraid not, unless his body is found, which is extremely unlikely,' said the vicar. 'In fact it's quite possible that he was never killed at all. Forgive me, but I think you allowed your imagination to run away with you over that. All you saw was a piece of rope, remember. If you had actually seen the man dead, or even wounded, well, that would be a different matter.'

'I heard my uncle threaten him. Isn't that enough?'

'My dear child, people threaten one another every day of the year, but they don't hang for it. Now listen to me. I am your friend, and you can trust me. If you ever become worried or frightened, I want you to come and tell me about it. Altarnun is only a few miles by the road. That's agreed between us, isn't it?'

'Thank you very much.'

'And now I'm going to drive you back to Jamaica Inn.'

The thought of returning was hateful to Mary, but it had to be faced. The night was fine; the dark clouds of the early evening had passed away, and the sky was bright with stars. It was a strange, exciting drive. The wind blew in Mary's face. The horse thundered along the hard white road, and the vicar made no attempt to control it. Mary saw that he was smiling. 'Go on,' he urged the animal, 'go on; you can go faster than this,' and his voice was low and excited, as if he were talking to himself. The effect was unnatural. Mary felt as if he were in another world and had forgotten her existence. He looked like a bird, bending forward in his seat; with his clothes blown by the wind, his arms were like wings. He might be any age. Then he smiled down at her, and was human again.

'I love these moors,' he said. 'If you knew them as well as I do, and had seen them in every type of weather, winter and summer, you would love them too. They go back a long way in time. Sometimes I think that they have lived on from another age. The moors were the first things to be made; afterwards came the forests and the valleys and the sea.'

Already Mary could see the tall chimneys of Jamaica Inn against the sky. The drive was ended, and the excitement left her. The old fear and hatred of her uncle returned. The vicar stopped his horse just before the yard, beside a grassy bank.

'There's no sign of anyone,' he said quietly. 'It's like a house of the dead. I'm going to look in at the window.'

She watched him go to the side of the house and he stood there for a few minutes looking. Then he made a sign to her to follow. 'There'll be no argument tonight with the landlord of Jamaica Inn.'

Mary followed the direction of his eyes and came forward to the window. Joss Merlyn sat at the table unconscious, his great legs stretched out on either side of him, his hat on the back of his head. He looked straight in front of him at the light, his eyes fixed like those of a dead man. A bottle lay with its neck broken on the table, and beside it an empty glass. The fire had burnt away to nothing.

Francis Davey pointed to the door. 'You can walk inside and go upstairs to bed. Your uncle will not even see you. Good night to you, Mary Yellan. If you're ever in trouble and need me, I shall be waiting for you at Altarnun.' Then he turned the corner of the house and was gone.

Chapter 8   Joss's Dreams

Joss Merlyn was drunk for five days. He was unconscious most of the time, and lay stretched out on a bed in the kitchen that Mary and her aunt had made up. He slept with his mouth wide open, and the sound of his breathing could be heard from the bedrooms above. At about five in the evening he would wake for about half an hour, shouting for drink and crying like a child. His wife went to him immediately, talking to him gently, holding a glass to his lips; and he looked wildly around, talking to himself and trembling like a frightened dog. Aunt Patience became another woman, showing a calm which Mary would not have believed her to possess. It seemed that every two months or so Joss Merlyn would have these periods of uncontrolled drinking. They were becoming more frequent, and Aunt Patience was never quite certain when they would happen.

On the fifth morning the wind dropped and the sun shone, and in spite of the adventure of a few days before, Mary decided to try the moors again. This time she made for the East Moor, walking towards Kilmar. With many hours of daylight to come, there was no danger of being lost.

Mary had walked for an hour or more before she stopped, her progress barred by a stream that divided and ran in different directions. It lay in a valley in the hills, and was surrounded by marshes. The country was not unknown to her; looking out beyond the green face of the tor ahead, she saw the great hand of Kilmar pointing its fingers to the sky. She was looking at Trewartha Moor once again, where she had wandered that first Saturday, but this time her face was turned to the south-east, and the hills looked different in the sunshine. The stream ran cheerfully over the stones. As Mary crossed it by a rough bridge, a group of horses came down the hill beyond and pushed into the stream to drink. Out of the corner of her eye she saw a man following them down the path, carrying a bucket in each hand. She was about to continue her walk when he waved a bucket in the air and shouted to her. It was Jem Merlyn. There was no time to escape, so she stood where she was until he came to her, looking just as his brother must have looked 20 years ago.

'So you've found your way to me, have you?' he said. 'I didn't expect you so soon, or I'd have made some bread in your honour. I haven't washed for three days and I've been living on potatoes. Here, take hold of this bucket.'

He pushed one of the buckets into her hand and ran down to the water after the horses. 'Come out of it!' he shouted. 'Dirtying my drinking water! Go on, you big black devil.'

He hit the largest of the horses with the end of the bucket, and they all ran back up the hill, kicking their feet in the air.

'What would you have done if you hadn't found me at home?' he said, wiping his face on his arm. Mary could not help smiling.

'I didn't even know you lived here, and I certainly never walked this way with the intention of finding you. I'd have turned left if I'd known.'

'I don't believe you. You started out with the hope of seeing me, and it's no use pretending anything different.'

He led the way up the path and, turning the corner, they came to a small grey house built on the side of the hill. There were some rough farm buildings at the back, and a piece of land for potatoes. She followed him in, bending her head under the low doorway. The room was small and square. Mary looked around her in disgust.

'Don't you ever do any cleaning?' she asked him. 'You ought to be ashamed of yourself. Leave me that bucket of water and find me a brush.' She set to work immediately. 'How long has your mother been dead?'

'Seven years this Christmas,' he answered. 'Because of my father being hanged and Matt drowned and Joss gone off to America and me growing up wild, she turned religious, and used to pray here by the hour, calling on the Lord. I couldn't bear that, so I ran away to sea. But the sea didn't suit my stomach, and I came back home. I found Mother very thin. "You ought to eat more," I said. But she wouldn't listen to me, so I went off again and stayed in Plymouth for a time, earning a little in my own way. I came back and found the place empty and the door locked. They told me my mother had died. She'd been buried three weeks . . . What's the matter?'

39

'It'll be a good thing when there's not a Merlyn left in Cornwall! It's better to have disease in a country than a family like yours. You and your brothers were born twisted and evil. Do you never think of what your mother must have suffered?'

Jem looked at her in surprise.

'Mother was all right. She never complained. She was used to us. How's the landlord of Jamaica Inn, then?'

'He's had too much to drink, like his father before him.'

'That'll be the ruin of Joss,' said his brother seriously. 'One day he'll kill himself with drink. The fool! Has anything been happening at Jamaica Inn?'

'We had Mr Bassat from North Hill last week.'

'You did? What did the magistrate have to say to you?'

'Uncle Joss was away from home. Mr Bassat was determined to come into the inn and search the rooms. He broke down the door at the end of the passage, but the room was empty. He seemed disappointed, and very surprised, and he rode away in a bad temper. He asked about you, as it happened, and I told him I had never seen you.'

Jem's face was without expression as she told her story, but when she came to the end of her sentence, and the mention of himself, he laughed. 'Why did you lie to him?' he asked.

'It seemed less trouble at the time. If I'd thought longer, no doubt I'd have told him the truth. You've got nothing to hide, have you?'

'Nothing much, except that the black horse you saw by the stream belongs to him. He was grey last week, and worth a small fortune to Mr Bassat. I'll get a few pounds for him at Launceston if I'm lucky. Come down and have a look at him.'

They went out into the sun. Then Jem spoke again.

'What did Mr Bassat expect to see at Jamaica Inn?'

Mary looked him straight in the eyes. 'You ought to know that better than I do,' she answered.

'It was lucky for Joss that everything had been moved,' he said quietly. 'It's only a matter of time before they catch him. All he does in self-defence is to get drunk, the fool.'

Mary said nothing. If Jem was trying to trap her by his openness, he would be disappointed.

'You must have a good view from that little room over the front door,' he said. 'Do they wake you from your sleep?'

'How do you know that's my room?' Mary asked quickly.

She saw the surprise in his eyes. Then he laughed. 'The window was wide open when I rode into the yard the other morning; I've never seen a window open at Jamaica Inn before.'

The excuse was hardly good enough for Mary, and a horrible suspicion came into her mind. Could it have been Jem who had hidden in the empty guest room that Saturday night? Something went cold inside her.

'What does it matter to you how much I know? All I think about is getting my aunt away from the place as soon as possible. As for your brother, he can drink himself to death for all I care. His life is his own, and so is his business. It's nothing to do with me.'

Jem whistled. 'So smuggling doesn't worry you after all? But supposing he were concerned with other things – supposing it were a question of life and death, and perhaps murder – what then?'

'I don't know what you mean,' said Mary.

He looked at her for a long time without speaking.

'Perhaps not,' he said at last, 'but you'll come to know, if you stay long enough. Why does your aunt look so pale? Ask her, next time the wind blows from the north-west . . . Why are you going? It's early yet; it won't be dark until after four. What's the matter with you?' He took her face in his hands and looked into her eyes. 'I believe you're frightened of me. You think I've got boxes of wine and spirits and tobacco in the little bedrooms above, and

41

that I'm going to show them to you, and then cut your throat. That's it, isn't it? We're a wild lot, we Merlyns, and Jem is the worst of us all. Is that what you're thinking?'

She smiled back at him in spite of herself. 'Something of the sort. But I'm not afraid of you; you needn't think that. I would even like you, if you didn't remind me so much of your brother.'

'I can't help my face,' he said, 'and I'm a much better-looking man than Joss; you must admit that.'

'Oh, you've confidence enough to make up for all the other qualities you lack, and I'll not argue about your face. Now let me go.'

'Are you coming to Launceston with me on Christmas Eve?'

'What will you be doing over at Launceston, Jem Merlyn?'

'Only selling Mr Bassat's horse for him, my dear. Say you'll come.'

'Supposing you are caught in Launceston with Mr Bassat's horse?'

'No one's going to catch me. Take a risk, Mary; don't you like excitement? You must be soft, down near Helford.'

'All right, Jem Merlyn. You needn't think that I'm afraid. I'd be just as happy in prison as at Jamaica Inn, anyway. How do we get to Launceston?'

'I'll take you there in my carriage, with Mr Bassat's horse tied up behind us.'

Mary was not afraid of him. To prove it, she would ride beside him to Launceston on Christmas Eve. She walked away up the hill without a backward look.

Darkness was falling as she crossed the road and entered the yard at Jamaica Inn. The door was opened by her aunt, who seemed pale and anxious.

'Your uncle has been asking for you all day. Where have you been?'

'I was walking on the moors – why should Uncle Joss ask for

42

me? He never has anything to say to me.'

'You must speak nicely to him. This is the bad time, when he's getting over it. He'll be bad-tempered — violent perhaps. You mustn't pay any attention to him at times like these. He's not really himself.'

The long evening passed, and still there was no call from the landlord. Mary's eyes closed in spite of herself. In a dream she heard her aunt whisper: 'I'm going to bed. Your uncle must have settled down for the night.' Mary felt sleep come over her. She dreamed that she was crossing the stream again. Her feet were wet. It was cold ... much too cold ... she must climb up the bank ... Mary opened her eyes and found that she was lying on the kitchen floor beside the ashes of the fire. The kitchen was cold. The light was low. She trembled, and stretched her stiff arms. Then she saw the door of the kitchen open very slowly, little by little. Suddenly it was thrown wide open, and Joss Merlyn stood there.

At first she thought that he had not seen her; his eyes were fixed on the wall in front of him. She bent low, her head beneath the level of the table, hearing nothing except the steady beating of her heart. Slowly he turned in her direction. When his voice came, it was hardly above a whisper: 'Who's there? What are you doing? Why don't you speak?' His face was grey. His eyes looked towards her without recognition. Mary did not move.

She waited, holding her breath. He moved forward into the room, his head bent, his hands feeling the air, and he crept slowly along the floor towards her until Mary could feel his breath on her face.

'Uncle Joss,' she said softly, 'Uncle Joss ...'

He stayed where he was, looking down at her, and then he leant forward and touched her. 'Mary? Is it you, Mary? Why don't you speak to me? Where have they gone? Have you seen them?'

'You've made a mistake, Uncle Joss,' she said. 'There's no one

43

here – only myself. Aunt Patience is upstairs. Are you ill? Can I help you?'

He looked around him in the half-light, searching the corners of the room.

'They can't frighten me,' he whispered. 'Dead men can't harm the living. It's dreams; all dreams! Their faces stand out like living things in the darkness, and I wake trembling. I'm thirsty, Mary; here's the key; go into the bar and find me something to drink.'

When she got back, he was sitting at the table with his head in his hands. At first she thought that he was asleep again, but at the sound of her footsteps he lifted his head. She put the bottle and the glass on the table in front of him. He filled the glass.

'You're a good girl. I'm fond of you, Mary. You've got sense, and you've got courage. They ought to have made you a boy.' He swallowed the drink, smiling foolishly. Then he pointed at the bottle. 'They pay gold for this. It's the best that money can buy. King George himself hasn't anything better. They can't catch me, Mary: I'm too clever; I've been at the game too long. There are over a hundred of us now, working towards the border from the coast. I've seen blood in my time, Mary, and I've seen men killed many times, but this game beats it all – it's running side by side with death.' He seized hold of Mary's arm. 'It's that cursed drink that makes a fool of me. I'm as weak as a rat when it has hold of me, you can see that. And I have dreams; I see things that frighten me. I've killed men with my own hands, pushed them under water with my feet, beaten them with rocks and stones, and I've never thought more about it – I've slept in my bed like a child. But when I've had too much to drink I see them in my dreams. I see their white-green faces in front of me, with their eyes eaten by fish; and some of them are torn, with the flesh hanging off their bones . . .'

His face was close to Mary's, his reddened eyes looking into hers, and his breath on her cheek. 'Did you never hear of wreckers before?' he whispered. 'I've seen men hanging on the ropes of their ships for safety, shouting in terror at the sight of the breaking waves. Just like flies they are, spread out on the ropes — little black dots of men. I've seen the ship break up beneath them, and the ropes break like thread, and all of them thrown into the sea, to swim for their lives. But when they reach the shore they're dead men, Mary.' He wiped his mouth on the back of his hand; his eyes never left her face. 'Dead men tell no stories, Mary.' She felt sick, and her hands and her feet were icy-cold. She could see the pale faces of the drowned men, their arms above their heads; she could hear the cries of fear. She trembled again.

She looked at her uncle, and saw that he had slipped forward in his chair, and his head had fallen on his chest. His mouth was wide open, and he breathed noisily as he slept. His arms rested on the table in front of him, and his hands were folded as if in prayer.

Chapter 9   Christmas Eve

On Christmas Eve the sky was cloudy and threatened rain. Mary leant out of the window, and the soft wet wind blew on her face. In an hour's time Jem Merlyn would be waiting for her on the moor, to take her to Launceston market. Whether she met him or not depended on herself, and she could not make up her mind. She had grown older in four days, and the face that looked back at her from her cracked mirror was pale and tired. There were dark rings under her eyes. Sleep came to her late at night, and she had no desire for food. For the first time in her life, she saw a likeness between herself and Aunt Patience. If she tightened her mouth and bit her lips, it could be Aunt Patience who stood there, with the straight brown hair framing her face. The habit of working her mouth was an easy one to catch, as was the continuous twisting of her hands. Mary turned away from the

45

mirror and began to walk up and down her small room. They shared a secret now, a secret that must never be spoken between them. Mary wondered how many years Aunt Patience had kept that knowledge to herself in silence. In her own way, Aunt Patience was a murderer too. She had killed by her silence.

There remained Jem Merlyn. He broke into her thoughts against her will, and she did not want him there. She had enough on her mind without Jem. He was too like his brother. His eyes, and his mouth, and his smile. She knew why Aunt Patience had made a fool of herself ten years ago. It would be easy enough to fall in love with Jem Merlyn. He was rough; he was rude; he was a thief and a liar. He stood for everything she feared and hated, but she knew she could love him. Jem Merlyn was a man, and she was a woman, and something inside her wanted him. She knew she would have to see him again. Today she would go to Launceston, and this time it was he who would answer her questions; he would realize that she was no longer afraid of the Merlyns, but could destroy them when she chose. And tomorrow – well, tomorrow could take care of itself. There was always Francis Davey and his promise; there would be peace and shelter for her in the house at Altarnun.

◆

This was a strange Christmas, she thought, as she walked across the East Moor. In the distance she saw a little group coming towards her – the horse, the cart, and two horses led behind. The driver raised his whip in a signal of welcome. Mary felt the colour in her face. He whistled as he came near, and threw a package at her feet. 'A happy Christmas to you,' he said. 'I had a silver piece in my pocket, so I had to spend it. There's a new hat for you.'

She had meant to be silent on meeting him, but this made it difficult. 'That's very kind of you,' she said, 'but I'm afraid you've wasted your money.'

'That doesn't worry me. I'm used to it,' and he looked at her in that cool way of his. 'You were here early. Were you afraid I'd go without you?'

She climbed up beside him. 'Mother and I used to drive into Helford once a week on market days. It all seems very long ago. It hurts me when I think of it, and how we used to laugh together, even when times were bad. You wouldn't understand that, of course. You've never cared for anything but yourself.'

They rode along in silence. Jem was playing with his whip. Mary looked out of the corner of her eye at his hands, and saw that they were long and thin; they had the same strength, the same sensitivity, as his brother's. These hands attracted her; the others frightened her. She realized for the first time that love and hate ran side by side; that the borderline was thin between them. The thought was an unpleasant one. Supposing this had been Joss beside her, ten, twenty years ago? She pushed the comparison to the back of her mind, fearing it. She knew now why she hated her uncle.

His voice interrupted her thoughts. 'What are you looking at?'

She lifted her eyes. 'I happened to notice your hands,' she said shortly; 'they are like your brother's . . . How far do we go across the moor? Isn't that the road over there?'

'We join it lower down and miss two or three miles of it. So you notice a man's hands, do you? I should never have believed it of you. You're a woman after all, then, and not a half-grown farm boy! Are you going to tell me why you have sat in your room for days, or do you want me to guess? Women love to be mysterious.'

'There's no mystery in it. You asked me last time we met why my aunt looked as she does. Well, I know now, that's all.'

'What are you going to do about it?'

Mary said: 'I haven't made up my mind. I have to consider Aunt Patience. You don't expect me to tell you, do you?'

'Why not? I'm not concerned with Joss.'

47

'You're his brother, and that's enough for me.'

'Do you think I'd waste my time working for my brother? He can put a rope round his own neck. I may have helped myself to some tobacco now and then, and I've smuggled goods, but I'll tell you one thing, Mary Yellan, and you can believe it or not as you like; I've never killed a man – yet.' He cracked the whip hard over the horse's head. 'So you think I wreck ships, do you, and stand on the shore and watch men drown? And then put my hands into their pockets afterwards, when they're swollen with water? It makes a pretty picture.'

Whether his anger was pretended or sincere she could not say, but his mouth was set firmly, and there was a flaming spot of colour high on his cheek.

'You haven't said yet that you don't.'

'If you believe it of me, why do you drive with me to Launceston?'

'Because of your bright eyes, Jem Merlyn! I ride with you for no other reason,' and she met his eyes with a directness that surprised him.

He laughed at that, and shook his head, and began whistling again; and suddenly there was a relaxed familiarity between them. The very directness of her words had deceived him. He suspected nothing of the weakness that lay behind them, and for the moment they were companions in spite of being man and woman.

They came now to the road, and as the horse increased speed the cart rolled along, with the two stolen horses running behind. It was a happy and rather heated party that reached Launceston that afternoon. Mary had thrown worry and responsibility to the winds and in spite of her determination in the morning she had given herself to enjoyment. Away from the shadow of Jamaica Inn her natural youth and high spirits returned. She laughed because he made her laugh; there was excitement in the air – a sense of

48

Christmas; the streets were filled with people; the little shops were bright and cheerful. This was a world that Mary loved. She wore the hat that Jem had given her and even allowed him to tie the ends under her chin. They had left the horse and carriage at the top of the town, and now Jem pushed his way through the crowd, leading his two stolen horses, Mary following close behind him. He led the way with confidence, making straight for the main square.

Before long a man pushed through the crowd and came up to the horses. His voice was loud and important. He kept hitting his boot with his whip, and then pointing to the horses. Mary imagined him to be a dealer. Soon he was joined by a little sharp-eyed man in a black coat, who now and again touched his arm and whispered in his ear.

Mary saw him look hard at the black horse that had belonged to Mr Bassat; he went up to him, and bent down and felt his legs. Then he whispered something in the ear of the loud-voiced man. Mary watched him, nervously.

'Where did you get this horse?' said the dealer, touching Jem on the shoulder. 'Never on the moors, not with that head and shoulders.'

'I bought him from old Tim Bray; you remember Tim? He sold his farm last year and went to Dorset. Tim always told me I'd get my money back on this horse. Have a look at him, won't you? But he's not going cheap, I'll tell you that. Look at those shoulders; there's quality for you! I tell you what, I'll take eighteen pounds for him.' The sharp-eyed man shook his head but the dealer was interested.

'Make it fifteen and we might do business,' he suggested.

'No, eighteen is my price, and no less.'

The dealer talked to his companion, and they appeared to disagree. 'All right,' the dealer said finally, 'I've no doubt you're right. Perhaps we would be wise to have nothing to do with it.

You can keep your horse,' he added to Jem. 'My friend doesn't like him. Take my advice and bring down your price. If you have him for long you'll be sorry.' And he pushed his way through the crowd, with the sharp-eyed man beside him, and they disappeared in the direction of the local hotel. Mary was glad to see them go.

Jem sold the other horse to a cheerful, honest-looking farmer. It began to get dark in the market square, and the lamps were lit. Mary was thinking of going back to the cart when she heard a woman's voice behind her.

'Oh, look James! Did you ever see such a beautiful horse in your life? He holds his head just like poor Beauty did. The likeness would be quite striking, only this animal of course is black. What a pity Roger isn't here. He's in his meeting. What do you think of him, James?'

Her companion said, 'Come on, Maria, I don't know anything about horses. The horse you lost was grey, wasn't it? This thing is black, coal black, my dear. Do you want to buy him?'

'It would be such a good Christmas present for the children. They've been begging poor Roger for another horse ever since Beauty disappeared. Ask the price, James, will you?'

The man came forward. 'Here, my good man,' he called to Jem, 'do you want to sell that black horse of yours? What is your price?'

'Twenty-five pounds,' said Jem. 'I'm not anxious to sell him.' The lady swept towards him. 'I'll give you thirty for him. I'm Mrs Bassat, from North Hill, and I want the horse as a Christmas present for my children. Mr Bassat is in Launceston now, but I want the horse to be a surprise to him as well. My man shall take the horse immediately, and ride him to North Hill before Mr Bassat leaves the town. Here's the money.'

Jem took off his hat to her. 'Thank you, madam,' he said. 'I hope Mr Bassat will be pleased. You'll find the horse very safe with children.'

'Oh, I'm certain he'll be very happy. Of course, the horse is not at all like the one we had stolen. Beauty was a fine horse, and worth a great deal of money. But this little animal is pretty enough, and will please the children. Come along, James; it's getting quite dark.'

Jem looked quickly over his shoulder, and touched on the arm a boy who stood behind him. 'Here,' he said, 'would you like to earn some money?' The boy showed that he would, his mouth open in surprise. 'Hold on to this horse, then, until the servant comes for him, will you? Here, take him. A happy Christmas to you!'

And he was away in a moment, walking quickly across the square, his hands in his pockets. Mary followed, ten yards behind. She struggled to hide her laughter, and was near to bursting when they got out of sight of the people.

'Jem Merlyn, you deserve to be hanged,' she said, when she could speak again. 'To stand there in the market square and sell that stolen horse back to Mrs Bassat herself! The hair on my head has gone grey with watching you.'

He threw back his head and laughed, and she could not help herself. Their laughter filled the street. Jem caught her hand. 'You're glad you came now, aren't you?'

They threw themselves into the crowded market, where Jem bought Mary gold rings for her ears. They sucked oranges beneath a striped tent, and had their fortunes told by an old woman. 'Do not trust a dark stranger,' she said to Mary, and they looked at each other and laughed again. 'There's blood on your hand, young man,' she told him. 'You'll kill a man one day.'

'What did I tell you on the cart this morning?' said Jem. 'There's no blood on my hands yet. Do you believe me now?' But she shook her head at him and would not say. Drops of rain fell on their faces, but they did not care. The wind rose.

Jem dragged Mary into the shelter of a doorway, his arms

around her shoulders, and he turned her face towards him, and kissed her. 'Do not trust a dark stranger,' he said, and he laughed, and kissed her again. The night clouds had come up with the rain, and it was dark in a moment.

'You don't want to ride on an open cart in this wind, do you? It's coming from the coast, and we'll be blown over on the high ground. We'll have to spend the night together in Launceston.'

'Very likely! Go and get the horse and cart, Jem, while this rain stops for the moment. I'll wait for you here.'

'You'll be wet to the skin on the Bodmin road! Pretend you're in love with me, can't you? You'd stay with me then.'

'Are you talking to me like this because I'm the bar girl at Jamaica Inn?'

'I like the look of you, and that's enough for any man. It ought to be enough for a woman, too.'

'Perhaps it is, for some. I'm just not made that way.'

'All right, I'll get the horse and cart, and take you home to your aunt, but I'll kiss you first, whether you like it or not.' He took her face in his hands. 'One for sorrow, two for joy! I'll give you the rest when you are more ready to accept them.'

Then he bent his head against the rain and she saw him disappear round the corner.

Mary waited, moving her feet and blowing on her hands. The long minutes passed, and still he did not come. Mary was cold and tired. At last she could bear it no longer, and she set off up the hill in search of him. The long street was empty, except for one or two people who sheltered in doorways as she had done. The rain was continuous, and the wind blew hard. There was nothing left now of the Christmas spirit.

The hotel looked welcoming enough, with its lighted windows, but there was no sign of the horse and cart. Mary's heart sank. Surely Jem had not started back without her? She paused for a moment, and then she went to the door and entered the hotel.

The hall seemed to be full of gentlemen, talking and laughing. Her country clothes and wet hair caused surprise, and a servant came up to her immediately and told her to leave. 'I've come in search of Mr Jem Merlyn,' said Mary firmly. 'He came here with a horse and cart. I'm sorry to trouble you, but I'm anxious to find him. Will you please ask if he's here?'

She turned her back on the little group of men who stood by the fire and watched her. Among them she recognized the dealer and the sharp-eyed man.

'If it's the dark one who tried to sell my friend a horse this afternoon, I can tell you about him,' said the little man, showing a row of broken teeth. Laughter came from the group by the fire.

She looked from one to the other. 'What do you have to say?'

'He was in the company of a gentleman only ten minutes ago,' answered the sharp-eyed man, still smiling, and looking at her rudely. 'With the help of some of us he was persuaded to enter a carriage that was waiting at the door. He was not keen at first, but a look from the gentleman appeared to decide him. No doubt you know what happened to the black horse? The price he was asking was undoubtedly high.'

His remark brought fresh laughter from the group by the fire. Mary looked steadily at the little sharp-eyed man.

'Do you know where he went?'

'No. And I'm afraid that your companion left you no parting message. But, it is Christmas. It's not pleasant weather outside. If you'd like to wait here until your friend returns, myself and these gentlemen will be happy to entertain you. Come in and rest, and forget him.'

Mary turned her back on him and went out through the door once more. As it closed behind her she could hear their laughter.

She stood in the empty market square with the wind and the rain for company. So the worst had happened, and the stolen horse had been recognized. There was no other explanation. Jem had gone. Did they hang men for stealing as well as for murder? She felt ill, and her brain was in confusion. She could make no plans. She supposed that Jem was lost to her now, anyway, and she would never see him again. The adventure was over.

There was no happiness left in Launceston any more; it was a cold, grey, hateful place. She walked along with the rain beating in her face, caring little where she went, or that 11 miles lay between her and her bedroom at Jamaica Inn. She walked on. Then out of the darkness she saw a carriage coming up the hill. Its progress was slow, with the full force of the wind against it. She watched it with dull eyes. It was passing her, when suddenly she ran after it and called to the driver wrapped up in a coat on the seat. 'Are you taking the Bodmin road? Have you a passenger inside?' The driver shook his head and whipped his horse, but before Mary could step to one side, an arm came out of the carriage window and a hand was laid on her shoulder. 'What does Mary Yellan do alone in Launceston on Christmas Eve?' said a voice from inside. The voice was gentle. A pale face looked out at her from inside the carriage; white hair and white eyes beneath the broad black hat. It was the Vicar of Altarnun.

◆

She watched his face in the darkness; his thin nose curved down like the beak of a bird, his lips narrow and colourless, pressed firmly together. He leant forward with his chin resting on a walking stick that he held between his knees. For the moment she could see nothing of his eyes: they were hidden by his short white eyelashes. Then he turned in his seat and looked at her, and the eyes that looked at her were white too, expressionless as glass.

'So we ride together for the second time,' he said, and his voice was soft and low, like the voice of a woman. 'Once more I have the good fortune to help you on your way. Well?' He looked steadily at her, and she found herself trying to give an explanation of her day. As before at Altarnun, there was something about him that made her sound like a fool, for she came out of the story badly – just another woman who had made herself cheap at Launceston market and had been left by the man of her choice to find her way home alone.

'What was the name of your companion?' he asked quietly; and she paused, awkward and uncomfortable, her sense of guilt stronger than ever.

'He was my uncle's brother.'

'You mean the brother knows nothing of the landlord's trade by night?' continued the gentle voice beside her. 'He is not of the company who bring the wagons to Jamaica Inn?'

'I don't know,' she said. 'I have no proof. He admits nothing. But he told me one thing: that he had never killed a man. And I believe him. He also said that my uncle was running straight into the hands of the law, and that they would catch him before long. He surely would not say that if he were one of the company. You told me before that you knew Mr Bassat. Perhaps you have some influence with him. Could you persuade him to deal kindly with Jem Merlyn, when the time comes? After all, he is young; he could start life again. It would be easy for a man in your position.'

'I know Mr Bassat only very slightly,' he told her gently. 'Once or twice we have spoken of matters which concern our two villages. It is hardly likely that he would pardon a thief because of me, especially if the thief is guilty and happens to be the brother of the landlord of Jamaica Inn. How old are you?'

'Twenty-three.'

'You are very young, Mary Yellan,' he said softly; 'you are nothing but a chicken with the broken shell still around you. Women like you have no need to cry over a man met once or twice; and a first kiss is not a thing to be remembered. You will forget your friend with his stolen horse very soon. Come now, dry your eyes; you are not the first to cry over a lost lover.'

He treated her problem lightly. She wondered why he had not used the words of comfort expected from a priest. She remembered that last ride with him, when he had whipped his horse into a fever of speed, and how he had bent forward in his seat and had whispered under his breath words she had not understood. Again she felt something of the same discomfort, which she connected with his strange hair and eyes, as though his unusual appearance cut him off from the rest of the world.

'So I was right in my guess, and all has been quiet at Jamaica Inn?' he said after a while.

Immediately she remembered the full story of the past week, and the new knowledge that had come to her.

'Mr Davey,' she whispered, 'have you ever heard of wreckers?' It was too dark to see his face, but she heard him swallow. 'My uncle is one of them. He told me so himself.' Still her companion made no reply, and she went on in a whisper. 'They are in it, every one of them, from the coast to the river bank, all those men I saw that first Saturday in the bar at the inn – the sailors, the thieves, the pedlar with the broken teeth. They've murdered women and children with their own hands; they've held them under water; they've killed them with rocks and stones. Those are death wagons that travel the road by night, and the goods they carry are from wrecked ships, bought at the price of blood. And that's why my uncle is feared and hated by the people in the houses and farms, and why all doors are barred against him, and why the coaches drive past the inn in a cloud of dust. They suspect what they cannot prove. There, Mr Davey; now you know the truth about Jamaica Inn.'

'So the landlord talks when he has had too much drink?' he said, and it seemed to Mary that his voice lacked something of its usual gentle quality; but when she looked up at him his eyes looking back at her were as cold and expressionless as always.

'He talks, yes. That's how I know. And perhaps that's why I've

ITEM ON HOLD

Title: Jamaica Inn / Daphne Du Maurier ; retold by A.S.M. Ronaldson.

Author: Du Maurier, Daphne, 1907-1989.

Call Number: PE1126 .N43 D86 1999

Enumeration:

Chronology:

Copy: 1

Item Barcode:

Item Being Held For:

Patron: INTERLIBRARY LOANS

Patron Barcode:

Patron Phone: 250 762-5445 LOC 4293

Hold Expires: 22/01/2007

Pickup At: Kelowna Circulation Desk

stopped trusting people, God and even myself; and why I acted like a fool today in Launceston.'

The wind had increased in force. The carriage shook. There was no shelter now; the moor on either side was empty, and the clouds flew fast over the land. There was a salty wet smell to the wind that had come from the sea 15 miles away.

Francis Davey leant forward in his seat. 'We are coming to the turning that leads to Altarnun. The driver is going on to Bodmin and will take you to Jamaica Inn. I shall leave you at the turning and walk down to the village. Am I the only man to know your secret, or do I share it with the landlord's brother?'

'Jem Merlyn knows,' she said. 'We spoke of it this morning. He said little, though, and I know that he is not friendly with my uncle. Anyway, it doesn't matter now. Jem is going to prison for another crime.'

'And suppose he could save himself by telling about his brother, what then, Mary Yellan? There's a thought for you.'

Mary was surprised by this new idea. But the Vicar of Altarnun must have read her thoughts. 'That would be a relief to you and to him, no doubt, if he had never helped with the wrecking. But there is always the doubt, isn't there? And neither you nor I knows the answer. A guilty man does not usually tie the rope round his own neck.'

Mary made a helpless movement with her hands, and he laid his hand on her knee.

'I will tell you one thing to comfort you. A week from now will bring the New Year. The false lights have burnt for the last time, and there will be no more wrecks.'

'I don't understand you. How do you know this, and what has the New Year to do with it?'

He called the driver to stop the horse. 'I am returning tonight from a meeting in Launceston. Those of us present were informed that at last the Government is prepared to guard the coast. There will be watchers on the cliffs, and the paths now known only to men like your uncle and his companions will be followed by officers of the law. There will be a chain across England, Mary, that will be very hard to break. Now do you understand?' He opened the door of the carriage and stepped out into the road. 'Your troubles are over. Tomorrow is Christmas Day, and the bells at Altarnun will be ringing for peace. I shall think of you.' He waved his hand to the driver, and the carriage went on without him.

◆

There were still 3 miles to go, and those miles were the wildest of all. She sat in the corner of the carriage. Through the open window, travelling down on the wind, she heard a shot, and a distant shout and a cry. The voices of men came out of the darkness. She leant out of the window. The road rose steeply from the valley, and there in the distance were the tall chimneys of Jamaica Inn. Down the road came a company of men, led by one who carried a light before him as he ran. Another shot sounded, and the driver of the carriage slipped over in his seat and fell. The horse went towards the edge of the road like a blind thing. The carriage swung wildly, then was still. Somebody laughed; there was a whistle and a cry.

A face appeared at the carriage window, wild hair above the reddened eyes. The lips were parted to show white teeth. One hand held a light, the other a smoking gun; they were long, thin hands, things of beauty and sensitivity, though the rounded nails were dirty. Joss Merlyn laughed; then he pulled her out beside him on the road, holding the light above his head so that all could see her. There were ten or twelve of them standing in the road, with torn and dirty clothes, half of them as much the worse for drink as their leader, wild eyes rolling in their bearded faces; one or two had guns in their hands, or were armed with broken bottles, knives and stones. Harry the pedlar stood holding the horse's head, while face-down on the road lay the driver of the carriage, his arm bent under him, his body still. When they saw who she was, a shout of laughter broke from the men, and the pedlar put two fingers to his mouth and whistled.

The landlord seized her loose hair in his hand and twisted it like a rope. 'So it's you, is it? You've chosen to come back again?'

Mary said nothing. She looked from one to the other of the men in the crowd and they pushed in on her, laughing, pointing to her wet clothes and shouting insults.

'So you can't talk?' cried her uncle, and hit her across the face with the back of his hand. She put up an arm to protect herself, but he knocked it away and, holding her wrist, twisted it behind her back. She cried with the pain, and he laughed again.

'I'll get the better of you, if I kill you first. Do you think you can stand against me, with your monkey face and your rudeness . . . and what do you think you are doing at midnight, riding in a hired carriage, with your hair down your back?' He twisted her wrist again, and she fell. 'You're nothing but a common . . .'

'Leave me alone!' she cried. 'You have no right to touch me or speak to me. You're a murderer and a thief, and the law knows it too. The whole of Cornwall knows it. Your game is over, Uncle Joss. I've been to Launceston today to inform against you.'

A loud cry came from the group of men; they pressed forward, shouting at her and questioning, but the landlord swore at them, waving them back.

'Get back, you fools! Can't you see she's trying to save herself by lies?' he thundered. 'How can she give information about me when she knows nothing? She's never walked the 11 miles to Launceston. Look at her feet. She's been with a man somewhere down the road, and he sent her back on wheels. Get up!' He pulled her to her feet. Then he pointed to the sky, where the low clouds were blown by the wind and a single star shone. 'Look there! There's a break in the sky, and the wind's going east. There'll be more wind still, and a wild grey morning on the coast in six hours' time. We'll waste no more time here. Come on, you lazy devils, don't you want to feel gold and silver run through your hands? Who'll come with me?'

A shout rose, and hands were raised in the air. One of the men burst into song, waving a bottle over his head. The pedlar pulled at the horse. Joss Merlyn stood for a moment, looking at Mary with a foolish smile, then he pulled her towards the carriage, threw her on the seat in the corner, and then, leaning out of the window, he shouted to the pedlar to whip the horse up the hill. His cry was repeated by the men who ran beside him, and some of them jumped onto the step and held onto the empty driver's seat and hit the horse with sticks. The animal sped up the hill in its fear, dragging the carriage behind it.

Jamaica Inn was all lit up. The doors and the windows were wide open. The landlord placed his hand over Mary's mouth and forced her back against the side of the carriage. 'You'd inform against me, would you? You'd run to the law, and have me swinging on a rope's end? All right then! You shall stand on the shore, Mary, and you shall watch for the daylight and the coming in of the tide. You know what that means, don't you? You know where I'm going to take you? You think you're not afraid of me, don't you? You hate me, with your pretty white face and your monkey eyes. Yes – I'm drunk! Tonight we shall all ride together proudly, perhaps for the last time. And you shall come with us, Mary – to the coast.'

He turned away from her, shouting to his companions, and the horse, frightened by his cry, moved even faster. The lights of Jamaica Inn disappeared into the darkness.

Chapter 10   The Wreck

It was a terrible journey of two hours or more to the coast, and Mary, hurt and shaken by her rough treatment, lay in the corner of the carriage, caring little about what happened to her. A sudden stillness, and the cold air blowing on her face through the open carriage window, brought her back to the world.

She was alone. The men had gone, taking their light with them. The carriage had been stopped in a narrow valley with high banks on either side, and the horse had been taken away. The valley appeared to slope down sharply, the track becoming rough and broken, but Mary could see only for a few yards. She tried the handle of the carriage door, but it was locked. Then she listened. Carried up towards her on the wind came the sound of the sea. The valley clearly led down to the shore. Mary trembled. Somewhere in the darkness below, her uncle and his companions were waiting for the tide.

Mary considered the size of the window. The door was locked, she knew, but she might force her body through the narrow window frame. She struggled and pushed, and then finally she lost her balance and fell to the ground below.

The drop was nothing, but the fall shook her and she felt blood run down her side where the window had caught her. She gave herself a moment to rest, and then she dragged herself to her feet and began to move uncertainly along the track, in the dark shelter of the bank. She had not yet formed a plan, but, with her back turned away from the sea, she would be putting distance between herself and the men. This track, leading upwards and to the left, would take her to the high ground above the beach.

She felt her way along the path, sometimes almost falling on loose stones, her hair blowing into her eyes. Turning a sharp corner, she put up her hands to push back the loose curls from her eyes, and because of this she did not see a man kneeling against the bank with his back towards her, his eyes watching the track ahead. She came against him, knocking the breath from his body, and he, taken by surprise, fell with her, crying out in fear and anger. They fought on the ground, her hands tearing at his face, but he was too strong for her. He leant on her, breathing heavily, and then he looked closely at her, showing broken yellow teeth. It was Harry the pedlar.

He expected her to cry or struggle but when she did neither, he moved his weight on to his arm and smiled at her in an ugly way. 'Didn't expect to see me, did you? Thought I was down on the shore with the landlord and the rest! But now you're here, I'll make you very welcome.' He was smiling still. She moved quickly, striking out at him, and hit him hard on the chin. In a second she had struggled from under him and pulled herself to her feet. She searched for a stone to throw at him, but finding nothing but loose earth and sand, she scattered this in his face and eyes, so that he was blinded for a moment. Then she turned again, and began to run like a hunted thing up the twisting track, her mouth open, her hands outstretched, falling over the stones in the path, all sense of direction gone, her one idea to escape from Harry the pedlar.

A wall of mist closed in on her, blocking out the distant line of bushes at which she had been aiming, and she stopped immediately, knowing the danger of low cloud, and how it might deceive her. Progress now was slow, but she knew that she was increasing the distance between herself and the pedlar, which was the only thing that mattered. She had no idea of the time; it was three, perhaps four, in the morning, and the darkness would give no sign of breaking for many hours. Once more the rain came down through the curtain of mist, and it seemed as if she could hear the sea on every side of her and there was no escape from it. The breaking waves, though she could not see them, were somewhere out in the darkness, and to her surprise it seemed that they were on a level with her, not beneath her. This meant that the track must have been only a few yards from the sea itself. The high banks had cut off the sound of the waves. Just as she decided this, there was a break in the mist ahead of her. Directly in front of her were the high waves breaking on the shore.

After a time, when her eyes had become used to the shadows, she saw, grouped against a large rock on the beach, a small number of men, silently looking ahead into the darkness. Their stillness made them more threatening. She waited. They did not move.

The mist began to lift very slowly, showing the shape of the coastline. To the right, in the distance, where the highest part of the rocks sloped to the sea, Mary could just see a light. At first she thought it was a star. But then she realized with a shock that it was a false light placed there by her uncle and his companions. They waited, all of them, standing on the stones with the waves breaking beyond their feet. Mary watched with them. Then out of the cloud and darkness came another light in answer to the first. And now Mary could see the dark shape of a ship and the white sea boiling around it. The ship's light drew closer to the light on the rocks, like an insect flying into a flame. Mary could bear no more. She got to her feet and ran out across the beach, shouting and crying, waving her hands above her head, lifting her voice in her battle against the sea and the wind, which threw it back to her. Someone caught hold of her and forced her down on to the beach. She was stepped on and kicked. Her cries died away as a rough cloth covered her mouth; her arms were pulled behind her and tied together, the rope cutting into her flesh.

They left her then, with the waves sweeping towards her not 20 yards away, and as she lay there helpless, she heard the cry that had been hers become the cry of others, and fill the air with sound. This cry rose above the noise of the sea, and was seized and carried by the wind; and with the cry came the terrible sound of splitting and breaking wood. Mary saw the great black shape that had been the ship roll slowly on its side in two parts. From it little black dots fell one by one into the white sea.

A terrible sickness came over Mary and she closed her eyes, her face pressed into the stones. The men who had waited during the cold hours waited no more. They ran crazily backwards and forwards on the sand, shouting. They walked waist-deep in the waves, careless of danger, seizing the goods carried in on the tide. They were animals, fighting and pulling things away from one another. One of them lit a fire in the corner by the rocks, the flames burning strongly in spite of the rain. The goods from the sea were dragged across the beach and piled beside it. The fire spread a yellow light over the scene and threw long shadows over the sand where the men ran backwards and forwards.

When the first body was washed on to the shore they ran to it, searching among the remains with their hands, picking it as clean as a bone. There was no system in their work tonight. They robbed here and there, crazy with the success they had not planned – dogs at the heels of their master whose idea had proved so successful, whose power this was, whose greatness. They followed him where he ran among the breaking waves, the water streaming from him; he was larger and stronger than them all.

The tide turned, and there was a new coldness in the air. The sky and the sea turned grey. At first the men did not notice the change. And then Joss Merlyn himself lifted his great head; he shouted suddenly, calling the men to silence, pointing to the sky that was pale now. They paused, looking once more at the things which rose and fell in the sea; and then they all turned and began to run towards the entrance to the little valley, silent once more, their faces grey and frightened in the growing light. Success had made them careless. The day had broken; the world was waking up; night, that had been their friend, covered them no more.

It was Joss Merlyn who tore the cloth away from her mouth and pulled Mary to her feet. He threw her over his shoulder and ran across the beach to the entrance to the valley; and his companions, caught up already in fear, threw some of the goods they had seized from the sea on the backs of the horses tied up there. Their movements were feverish and fearful. The carriage, stuck in the bank halfway up the valley, could not be pulled out in spite of all their efforts. Some of them ran off, in different directions. Here on the coast, where every face was known, strangers would be noticed; but a wanderer could make his way alone, finding his own cover and his own path. These running men were cursed by those who remained struggling with the carriage, and now, through stupidity and fear, it was pulled from the bank in so rough a manner that it overturned, rolling over on one side and breaking a wheel.

There was a wild rush to the remaining farm wagon that had been left farther up the road, and to the already overloaded horses. Someone, still obedient to the leader, set fire to the broken carriage, whose presence beside the track meant danger to them all. A terrible fight broke out between man and man for possession of the farm wagon that might yet carry them away to safety. Those who carried guns now had the advantage, and the landlord, with his remaining supporter Harry the pedlar by his side, stood with his back to the wagon and shot into the crowd. This won the wagon for the landlord. The remaining men, frightened at the sight of the blood and the dying men, turned all at the same moment and scattered up the twisting track, anxious now to put a safe distance between themselves and their former leader. The landlord leant against the wagon holding the smoking, murderous gun, blood running freely from a cut beside his eye. Now that they were alone, he and the pedlar wasted little time. The goods that had been brought up the valley they threw on the wagon with Mary next to them. The main store was still down on the sand and washed by the tide. They dared not risk collecting it; there was simply no time. The two men who had been shot lay in the road beside the wagon. Their bodies bore witness, and must be destroyed. It was Harry the pedlar who dragged them to the fire. It was burning well; much of the carriage had disappeared already, though one red wheel stuck up above the blackened and broken wood.

Joss Merlyn led the remaining horses to the wagon, and without a word the two men climbed in and whipped them into action. Lying on her back, Mary watched the low clouds pass across the sky. Darkness had gone; the morning was wet and grey. From far away across the fields came the sound of church bells. She remembered suddenly that it was Christmas Day.

Chapter 11   Joss Plans to Escape

The square of glass was familiar to her. It was larger than the carriage window, and there was a crack across it that she remembered well. She kept her eyes on it, struggling with memory, and she wondered why she no longer felt the rain on her face and the steady current of wind. Mary cried, and turned her head restlessly from side to side; out of the corner of her eye she saw the brown, discoloured wall beside her, and the old nail-head where a picture had once hung.

She was lying in her bedroom at Jamaica Inn.

Now there was a face bending down to her, and she drew back, her hands in front of her, because the ugly mouth and broken teeth of the pedlar were still in her mind. Her hands were held gently, though, and the eyes that looked down at her, reddened like her own from crying, were watery and blue.

It was Aunt Patience.

'How long have I been lying here?' Mary asked, and she was

told that this was the second day. For a moment she was silent, considering this information. Then she sat up in bed and swung her legs to the floor, her head aching with the effort.

'What are you going to do?' Aunt Patience pulled at her nervously, but the young woman shook her off and began, slowly and painfully, to put on her clothes.

'Aunt Patience, I have gone through enough out of loyalty to you. You can't expect me to stand any more. Whatever Uncle Joss may have been to you once, he isn't human now. He's an animal, half crazy with drink and blood. Men were murdered by him on the coast; don't you understand? Men were drowned in the sea. I can see nothing else. I shall think of nothing else until my dying day.'

The door opened; the landlord of Jamaica Inn stood in the doorway. He looked tired and grey; the cut above his eye was still bright red. He was dirty and unwashed, and there were black shadows under his eyes.

'I thought I heard voices in the yard, but I saw no one. Did you hear anything?' Nobody answered. He sat down on the bed, his hands picking at the bedclothes, his eyes wandering from the window to the door.

'He'll come. He's sure to come. I've cut my own throat; I've disobeyed him. He warned me once, and I laughed at him; I didn't listen. I wanted to play the game on my own. It means death for us, for all three of us sitting here. We're finished, I tell you. Why did you let me drink? Why didn't you break every bottle in the house, and turn the key on me? I'd not have hurt you. Now it's too late; the end has come.'

He looked from one to the other of them, his reddened eyes hollow; the women looked back without understanding.

'What do you mean?' said Mary at last. 'Who are you afraid of? Who warned you?'

He shook his head, and his hands wandered to his mouth, the

fingers restless. 'No,' he said slowly, 'my secrets are still my own. But I tell you one thing – and you're in it now as much as Patience there – we have enemies on either side of us now. We have the law on one hand, and on the other . . .' He stopped himself, the old look beginning to return to his eyes once more. 'You'd like to know, wouldn't you? You'd like to run out of the house with the name on your lips. You'd like to see me hanged. All right, I don't blame you for it. But I saved you too, didn't I? Nobody touched you last night except myself, and I've not spoilt your pretty face. Let's get out of here. This room smells of decay.'

They followed him without a word. He led the way to the kitchen, where the door was locked and the window barred. The landlord pulled the wooden shutters closed too. Then he turned and faced the women.

'We've got to think out a plan. We've been sitting here for nearly two days now, like rats in a trap. And I've had enough, I tell you. I never could play that sort of game.'

His wife crept over to him and touched him on the arm, passing her tongue over her lips.

'Well, what is it?' he said wildly.

'Why can't we creep away now, before it's too late? We'd be in Launceston and then out of the area in a few hours. We could travel by night. We could head east where we'd be safe.'

'You fool!' he shouted. 'Don't you realize that there are people on the road between here and Launceston who think I'm the devil himself – who are only waiting for their chance to charge me with every crime in Cornwall? Everybody round here knows by now what happened on the coast on Christmas Eve, and if they see us running away they'll have the proof. Don't you think I've wanted to get away and save myself? No, we've got one chance – one single chance in a million. We've got to lie quiet. If we stay here at Jamaica Inn it may confuse them. They've got to look for proof. They've got to get sworn proof before they lay hands on us. Oh, yes, the ship's there with her back broken on the rocks, and piles of things lying on the sand ready to take away. They'll find two burnt bodies, and a pile of ashes. Many of us will be suspected, but where's the proof? Answer me that. I was here that night with my family!'

'You've forgotten one thing, haven't you?' said Mary.

'No, my dear, I have not. The driver of that carriage was shot not a quarter of a mile down the road outside. You were hoping we'd left the body there, weren't you? The body travelled with us to the coast and it lies now, if I remember rightly, beneath a 10-foot bank of sand. Of course, someone is going to miss him. I'm prepared for that; but as they'll never find his carriage it does not matter much. Perhaps he was tired of his wife and has driven to Penzance. They can look for him there.'

He threw back his head and laughed; but his laugh was cut short in the middle, his mouth shut like a trap, his face as white as a sheet. 'Listen,' he whispered, 'listen . . .'

They followed the direction of his eyes, which were fixed on the crack of light that came through the shutters. Something was knocking gently at the kitchen window . . . knocking lightly, softly at the glass. There was no other sound in the kitchen except for the frightened breathing of Aunt Patience, whose hand crept along the table towards Mary. The landlord stood completely still for a moment. Then he bent forward until his fingers reached the gun that stood against the chair, never once taking his eyes from the shutters. He jumped forward, tearing the shutters open. A man stood outside the window, his face pressed against the glass, his broken teeth showing in a twisted smile. It was Harry the pedlar. Joss Merlyn swore, and threw open the window. 'Come inside, can't you? Do you want to be shot, you fool? Unlock the door, Mary.' She did so without a word. 'Well, have you brought news?' asked the landlord.

The pedlar pointed over his shoulder. 'The country's wild

with anger; they're crazy for blood and justice. There'll only be one end to this storm, Joss, and you know the name for it, don't you?' He made a sign with his hands across his throat. 'We've got to run,' he said. 'It's our only chance. The roads are poison, and Bodmin and Launceston worst of all. I'll keep to the moors; it'll take me longer, I know that, but what does that matter if you save yourself from hanging?'

'So you'll give up, Harry, will you? Run like a beaten dog? Have they proved it was us? Tell me that. Or are you worried about your soul?'

'Curse my soul, Joss; it's common sense I'm thinking of. This part of the country is dangerous, and I'll leave while I can. I've stayed by you, haven't I? I've come out here today, risking death, to give you warning. I'm not saying anything against you, Joss, but it was your stupidity that brought us to this, wasn't it? You made us crazy like yourself, and led us to the coast on an adventure that none of us had planned. We took a chance in a million – and succeeded. Too well. We became stupid with excitement, left a hundred tracks scattered on the sand. And whose fault was it? Why, yours, I say!' He banged the table, his yellow face pushed close to the landlord's.

Joss Merlyn considered him for a moment, and when he spoke his voice was dangerous and low. 'So you blame me, do you, Harry? You're like the rest of your kind when the luck of the game turns against you. Run, then, if you like; run to the river bank like a beaten dog. I'll fight the world alone!'

The pedlar forced a laugh. 'We can talk, can't we, without cutting each other's throats? I've not gone against you; I'm on your side still. We were all crazy that night, I know that. Let's leave it alone, then; what's done is done. Our men are scattered, and we needn't worry about them. They'll be too frightened to show their heads. That leaves you and me, Joss. We've been in this business, the pair of us, deeper than most, and the more we help each other, the better it'll be for us both. Now then, that's why I'm here, to talk and see what we ought to do.'

The landlord watched him calmly. 'Just what are you aiming at, Harry?' he said, filling his pipe.

'I'm not aiming at anything. I want to make things easier for all of us. We've got to go, unless we want to hang. But it's like this, Joss; I don't see the fun of going empty-handed. There are a lot of things we put in the store room two days ago. That's right, isn't it? It belongs to all of us who worked for it on that night. But there's none of them left to claim it except you and me. I'm not saying that there's much of value there, but I don't see why some of it shouldn't help us out of the area, do you?'

The landlord blew a cloud of smoke into his face. 'So you didn't come back to Jamaica Inn because of my sweet smile alone, then? I was thinking you were fond of me, and wanted to hold my hand.'

The pedlar smiled, and changed his position on his chair. 'All right – we're friends, aren't we? There's no harm in plain speaking. The things are here, and it'll take two men to move it. The women can't do it. What's against you and me making a deal?'

The landlord thoughtfully smoked his pipe. 'And supposing there's nothing here, after all? Supposing I've got rid of it already? I've been sitting here for two days, you know, and the coaches pass my door. What then, Harry boy?'

The smile went from the face of the pedlar. 'What's the joke? Do you play a double game up here at Jamaica Inn? You'll find it hasn't paid you, if you have. You've been clever at this trade, month in, month out; too clever, some of us thought, for the small profit we made out of it – we, who took most of the risks. And we didn't ask you how you did it. Listen here, Joss Merlyn; do you take your orders from someone above you?'

The landlord was on him like a flash. He hit him on the chin, and the man went over backwards onto his head. He rolled over onto his knees, but the landlord towered above him, his gun pointing at his throat.

'Move, and you're a dead man,' he said softly, as Harry looked up at his attacker, his little eyes half closed. 'Now we can talk, you and I.' He leant once more against the table, while the pedlar continued to kneel on the floor. 'You didn't come here tonight to warn me; you came to see what you could get out of the wreck. You didn't expect to find me here, did you? You thought it would be Patience here, or Mary; and you would frighten them easily, wouldn't you, and reach for my gun where it hangs on the wall, as you've often seen? You little rat, Harry, do you think I didn't see it in your eyes when I threw back the shutters and saw your face at the window? Do you think I didn't see your surprise? Very well, then. We'll make a deal, as you suggest. I've changed my mind, my loving friend, and with your help we'll take the road. There are things in this place worth taking, and I can't load them alone. Tomorrow is Sunday, and a day of rest. Not even the wrecking of 50 ships will drag the people around here from their knees. There'll be prayers offered for poor sailors who suffer because of the devil's work, but they'll not go looking for the devil on a Sunday.

'Twenty-four hours we have, Harry my boy, and tomorrow night when you've broken your back loading my property into the farm wagon and kissed me goodbye – why, then you can go down on your knees and thank Joss Merlyn for letting you go free with your life.'

He raised his gun again, bringing it close to the man's throat. The pedlar cried out, showing the whites of his eyes. The landlord laughed.

'Come on,' he said, 'do you think I'm going to play with you all night? Open the kitchen door, and turn to the right, and walk down the passage until I tell you to stop. Your hands have been waiting to explore the goods brought from the shore, haven't they, Harry? You shall spend the night in the store room among them all.' Pressing his gun into the pedlar's back, he pushed him out of the kitchen and down the dark passage to the store. The door had been mended with new wood and was stronger than before.

After he had turned the key on his friend, the landlord returned to the kitchen.

'I thought Harry would turn soon,' he said. 'I've seen it coming in his eyes for weeks. He'll fight on the winning side, but he'll turn against you when your luck changes. He's jealous of me. They're all jealous of me. They knew I had brains, and they hated me for it. You'd better get your supper and go to bed. You've a long journey to make tomorrow night, and I warn you here and now it won't be an easy one.'

Mary looked at him across the table. Tired as she was, because all that she had seen and done weighed heavily on her, her mind was full of plans. Some time, somehow, before tomorrow night, she must go to Altarnun. Once there, her responsibility was over. Action would be taken by others. It would be hard for Aunt Patience, hard for herself at first, perhaps, but at least justice would win. It would be easy enough to clear her own name, and her aunt's. The thought of her uncle standing as he would with his hands tied behind him, powerless for the first time and for ever, was something that gave her great pleasure. She dragged her eyes away from him. 'I'll have no supper tonight,' she said.

He crossed into the hall as she climbed the stairs, and he followed her to the room over the front door. 'Give me your key,' he said, and she handed it to him without a word. He stayed for a moment, looking down at her, and then he bent low and laid his fingers on her mouth.

'I like you, Mary. You've got spirit still, and courage, in spite of all the rough treatment I've given you. I've seen it in your eyes tonight. If I'd been a younger man I'd have fallen in love with you – and won you too, and ridden away with you. You know that, don't you?' He lowered his voice to a whisper. 'There's danger for me ahead. Never mind the law. The whole of Cornwall can come running at my heels and I shall not care. It's other things I have to watch for – footsteps, Mary, that come in the night and go again, and a hand that is waiting to strike me down. We'll put the river between us and Jamaica Inn,' he said; and then he smiled, the curve of his mouth painfully familiar to her like something from her past. He shut the door on her, and turned the key.

She went then to her bed, and sat on it. And she began to cry, softly and secretly, the tears tasting bitter as they fell on her hand.

Chapter 12   To Altarnun

She had fallen asleep where she lay, without undressing, and her first conscious thought was that the storm had returned. She was awake immediately, and she waited for the sound that had woken her to come again. It came in a moment, a handful of earth thrown against the window from the yard outside.

It was Jem Merlyn standing below in the yard. He whispered up to her, 'Come down to the door here, and open it for me.'

She shook her head. 'I can't – I'm locked in my room.' He looked back at her, confused, and examined the house as if it might offer some solution of its own. He ran his hand along the wall, feeling for old nails that might once have been used for training climbing plants, and would now give him a foothold of a sort. Swinging himself up to the low roof over the front door, he was able to pull himself up to the level of her window.

'I shall have to talk to you here,' he said. 'Come closer where I can see you.' She knelt on the floor of her room, her face at the window, and they looked at each other without speaking. He looked tired, and his eyes were hollow like those of one who has not slept. There were lines around his mouth that she had not noticed before, and he did not smile.

'I'm sorry,' he said at last. 'I left you alone without excuse at Launceston on Christmas Eve. You can forgive me or not. But the reason for it – that I can't give you. I'm sorry.'

She was hurt by his manner. His coldness upset her, and she hoped that he could not see the disappointment in her face. He did not even ask how she had returned that night.

'Why are you locked in your room?'

Her voice was flat and dull when she replied. 'My uncle fears that I may wander in the passage and discover his secrets.'

'Where is he?'

'He's going to spend the night in the kitchen. He's afraid of something, or someone; the windows and doors are barred, and he has his gun.'

Jem laughed bitterly. 'I don't doubt he's afraid. He'll be even more frightened before many hours have passed, I can tell you that. I came here to see him, but if he is sitting there with a gun across his knee I shall come again tomorrow, when the shadows have gone.'

'Tomorrow may be too late.'

'What do you mean?'

'He intends to leave Jamaica Inn tonight.'

'Are you telling me the truth?'

'Why should I lie to you now?'

Jem was silent. The news had clearly come as a surprise to him. She was thrown back now on her old suspicion of him. He was the visitor expected by her uncle, and therefore hated by him and feared. The face of the pedlar returned to her, and his words, that had stung Joss Merlyn to anger: 'Listen here, Joss Merlyn, do you take your orders from someone above you?' The man whose

75

brains made use of the landlord's strength, the man who had hidden in the empty room . . .

Leaning forward suddenly, he looked into her face and touched the long cut that ran from her forehead to her chin. 'Who did these?' he said, turning now to the mark on her cheek. She paused a moment, and then answered him.

'I got them on Christmas Eve.'

The look in his eye told her that he understood, and had knowledge of the evening, and because of it was here now at Jamaica Inn.

'You were with them, on the shore?' he whispered. 'Why did you go with them?'

'They were crazy with drink. I don't think they knew what they were doing. I could no more have stood against them than a child. There were ten of them or more, and my uncle . . . he led them. He and the pedlar. If you know about it, why do you ask me? Don't make me remember. I don't want to remember.'

'How much did they hurt you?'

'You can see for yourself. I tried to escape and I hurt my side. They caught me again, of course. They tied my hands and feet, and tied a cloth over my mouth so that I could not cry out. I saw the ship come through the darkness, and I could do nothing – alone there in the wind and the rain. I had to watch them die.'

She stopped, her voice trembling, her face in her hands. He made no move towards her; and she felt him far from her, wrapped in secrecy. She felt lonelier than ever.

'Was it my brother who hurt you most?' he said after a while.

It was too late; it did not matter now. 'I've told you he was very drunk. You know, better than I perhaps, what he can do then.'

'Yes, I know.' He paused for a moment, and then he took her hand. 'He shall die for this.'

'His death will not bring back the men he has killed.'

'I'm not thinking of them now.'

'If you're thinking of me, don't waste your sympathy. I can deal with it in my own way. I've learnt one thing – to depend on myself.'

'What do you intend to do?'

'He expects me to go with him, and Aunt Patience as well. If I asked you to do something, how would you answer me?'

He smiled then, for the first time, as he had done in Launceston, and her heart warmed, encouraged at the change.

'How can I tell?' he said.

'I want you to go away from here.'

'I'm going now.'

'No, I mean away from the moors – away from Jamaica Inn. I want you to tell me you won't return here. I can stand up against your brother; I'm in no danger from him now. I don't want you to come here tomorrow. Please promise me you'll go away.'

'What have you got in mind?'

'Something which does not concern you, but might bring you into danger. I can't say any more. I would rather you trusted me.'

'Trust you? Of course I trust you. It's you who won't trust me, you little fool.' He laughed silently, and bent down to her, putting his arms round her, and kissed her then as he had kissed her in Launceston, but with anger.

'Play your own game by yourself, then, and leave me to play mine. If you must be a boy, I can't stop you, but keep that face, which I have kissed and shall kiss again, away from danger. You don't want to kill yourself, do you? I have to leave you now; it will be light in less than an hour. And if both our plans go wrong, what then? Would you mind if you never saw me again? No, of course you wouldn't care. You'll marry a farmer one day, or a small tradesman, and live quietly among your neighbours. Don't tell them you once lived at Jamaica Inn, or had a horse thief make love to you. They'd shut their doors against you. Goodbye – and good luck to you.'

He lowered himself to the ground. She watched him from the window, waving to him, but he had turned and gone without looking back at her, crossing the yard like a shadow. Morning would soon be here; she would not sleep again.

She sat on her bed, waiting for her door to be unlocked; and she made her plans for the evening to come. She must act as if she were prepared to make the planned journey with the landlord and Aunt Patience. Later, she would make some excuse – a desire to rest in her room before the journey, perhaps – and then would come the most dangerous moment of her day. She would have to leave Jamaica Inn secretly and run to Altarnun. Francis Davey would understand; time would be against them, and he would have to act quickly. She would then return to the inn, and hope that her absence had remained unnoticed. That was the risk. If the landlord went to her room and found her gone, her life would be worth nothing. She must be prepared for that. No excuse would save her then. But if he believed her to be sleeping, the game would continue. They would make preparations for the journey; they might even climb into the wagon and come out on the road. After that, her responsibility would end. Whatever happened next would be in the hands of the Vicar of Altarnun. Beyond this she could not think, nor had she any great desire to look ahead.

◆

When she had helped them clear the midday meal away and had persuaded her aunt to pack a basket of food for the journey, she turned to her uncle and spoke to him.

'If we are to travel tonight, would it not be better if Aunt Patience and I rested now during the afternoon, so we could start out fresh on the journey? There will be no sleep for any of us tonight.'

'You may rest if you like. There'll be work for both of you later. You're right when you say there will be no sleep for you tonight. Go, then; I shall be glad to get rid of you for a time.'

Mary entered her own little room and closed the door, turning the key. Her heart beat fast at the thought of adventure. It was nearly 4 miles to Altarnun by road, but she could walk the distance in an hour. If she left Jamaica Inn at four o'clock, when the light was failing, she would be back again soon after six; and the landlord would be unlikely to come to wake her up before seven. She had three hours, then, in which to play her part. She would climb out of the window and drop to the ground, as Jem had done. She sat by the window, looking out on the empty yard and the high road where no one ever passed, waiting for the clock in the hall to strike four.

When it struck at last, the sound rang out in the silence. Every second was important to her now, and she must waste no time in going. She climbed through the window. The jump was nothing, as she had thought. She looked up at Jamaica Inn. It looked evil in the half-darkness, the windows barred; she thought of the terrible things the house had witnessed, the secrets now shut up behind its walls; and she turned away from it as from a house of the dead, and went out on the road.

Darkness fell as she walked. She came at last to where the roads divided, and she turned to her left, down the steep hill to Altarnun.

The vicar's house was silent. There were no lights there. She turned back towards the church. Francis Davey would be there, of course! It was Sunday. She stopped for a moment, uncertain what to do. Then the gate opened and a woman came out into the road, carrying flowers.

She looked hard at Mary, knowing her to be a stranger, and would have passed her by with a 'good night', but Mary turned. 'Forgive me,' she said. 'I see you have come from the church. Can you tell me if Mr Davey is there?'

'No, he is not,' said the woman; and then, after a moment, 'Did you want to see him?'

'Very urgently,' said Mary. 'Can you help me?'

The woman looked at her strangely, and then she shook her head firmly.

'I'm sorry,' she said. 'The vicar's away. He went to hold a service in another village, many miles from here. He is not expected back in Altarnun tonight.'

Chapter 13   Murder at Jamaica Inn

At first Mary looked at the woman in disbelief.

'But that's impossible. Surely you're mistaken?'

'The vicar has left. He rode away after dinner. I ought to know: I am his housekeeper.'

Mary wondered hopelessly what she could do now. To come to Altarnun and then return without help to Jamaica Inn was impossible. She could not place confidence in the village people, nor would they believe her story. She must find someone with power — someone who knew something of Joss Merlyn and Jamaica Inn.

'Who is the nearest magistrate?' she said at last.

The woman considered the question. 'Well, the nearest would be Mr Bassat over at North Hill, and that must be over 4 miles from here — perhaps more, perhaps less. I can't say for certain, for I've never been there. You surely don't intend to walk out there tonight?'

'I must. There is nothing else for me to do. I must waste no time, either. I'm in great trouble now, and only your vicar or a magistrate can help me.'

'You'd better stay here and wait for the vicar, if you can.'

'That's impossible,' said Mary, 'but when he does return, could you tell him perhaps that . . . But wait; if you have pen and paper, I'll write him a note of explanation. That would be better still.'

'Come into my house here, and you may write what you like. I can take the note to his house.'

Mary followed the woman to her house. Time was slipping away fast. Her uncle would take warning from the fact that she had run away, and leave the inn before the intended time. And then her effort would have been for nothing.

Mary wrote with the speed of hopelessness. Then she folded the note and gave it to the woman by her side. So she set out on a walk of 4 miles or more to North Hill.

She had placed such trust in Francis Davey that it was hard to realize that he had failed her. He had not known, of course, that she needed him. She was anxious about Aunt Patience, and the thought of her setting out on the journey like a trembling dog tied to its master made Mary run along the empty road. She came at last to big gates and the entrance to a driveway. This must be North Hill, and this house must belong to the magistrate. In the distance a church clock struck seven. She had been away from Jamaica Inn for about three hours already. Her fear returned as she came to the house. She swung the great bell and waited. After some time she heard footsteps inside, and the door was opened by a servant. 'I have come to see Mr Bassat on very urgent business,' she told him. 'The matter is of the greatest importance, or I would not come at such an hour, and on a Sunday night.'

'Mr Bassat left for Launceston this morning,' answered the man. 'He was called away at short notice, and he has not yet returned.'

This time Mary could not control herself, and a cry of hopelessness escaped her.

'I have come a long way,' she said, with great feeling, as if by the strength of her need for him she could bring the magistrate to her side. 'If I do not see him, something terrible will happen, and a great criminal will escape the hands of the law. You are looking at me strangely, but I am speaking the truth. If only there were someone I could turn to . . .'

'Mrs Bassat is at home,' said the man with interest. 'Perhaps she will see you, if your business is as urgent as you say. Follow me, will you, to the library?'

Mary crossed the hall in a dream, knowing only that her plan had failed again, through chance alone, and that she was now powerless to help herself. The library, with its bright fire, seemed unreal to her, and her eyes were not used to the light that met them. A woman, whom she recognized immediately as the lady who had bought the horse in Launceston market square, was sitting in a chair in front of the fire. She looked up in surprise when Mary was shown into the room.

Mrs Bassat rose to her feet. 'What can I do for you?' she said kindly. 'You look pale and tired. Won't you sit down?'

Mary shook her head impatiently. 'Thank you, but I must know when Mr Bassat is returning home.'

'I have no idea,' replied his wife. 'He had to leave this morning at a moment's notice, and, to tell you the truth, I am really anxious about him. If this innkeeper decides to fight, as he is certain to do, Mr Bassat may be wounded, in spite of the soldiers.'

'What do you mean?' said Mary quickly.

'He has set out on a highly dangerous piece of work. Your face is new to me, and I suppose you are not from North Hill, or you would have heard of the man Merlyn who keeps an inn on the Bodmin road. Mr Bassat has suspected him for some time of terrible crimes, but it was not until this morning that the full proof came into his hands. He left immediately for Launceston to get help, and he intends to surround the inn tonight, and seize the people inside. He will go well armed, of course, and with a large body of men, but I shall not rest until he returns.'

'I came here to warn Mr Bassat that the landlord intends to leave the inn tonight, and so escape justice. I have proof of his guilt, which I did not believe Mr Bassat to possess. You tell me that he has already gone, and perhaps even now is at Jamaica Inn. Therefore I have wasted my time in coming here.'

Mary sat down then, her hands folded, and looked unseeing into the fire. She had come to the end of her strength and for the moment she could not look into the future. All that her tired mind could tell her was that her journey this evening had been for nothing.

'I have done a very stupid thing in coming here,' she said miserably. 'I thought it clever, but I have only succeeded in making a fool of myself and of everyone else. My uncle will discover that my room is empty, and guess that I have informed against him. He will leave Jamaica Inn before Mr Bassat arrives.'

Mrs Bassat came towards her. 'You have been placed in a terrible position,' she said kindly, 'and I think you are very brave to come here tonight, all those lonely miles, to warn my husband. The question is: what do you want me to do now? I will help you in any way you think best.'

'I can think of nothing but my poor aunt, who at this moment may be suffering terribly. I must know what is happening at Jamaica Inn, if I have to walk back there myself tonight.'

'But you cannot possibly walk back there now, alone. I will order the carriage, and Richards will go with you. He can be trusted completely, and will carry guns for your protection. If there is fighting in progress, you need not go near the inn until it is over.'

In a quarter of an hour the carriage drove up to the door, with Richards in charge. Mary recognized him as the servant who had ridden with Mr Bassat to Jamaica Inn before. He wanted to know everything, of course, but she gave short answers to his questions, and did not encourage him. The horse and carriage quickly covered the miles that Mary had walked alone.

'We shall find them there before us, as likely as not,' Richards told Mary. 'It will be a good thing for the neighbourhood when he's in prison. It's a pity we were not here sooner; there'll have been some excitement in taking him, I expect.'

'Little excitement if Mr Bassat finds his man has escaped,' said Mary quietly. 'Joss Merlyn knows these moors like the back of his hand.'

'My master was born here, just as the landlord was,' said Richards. 'If it comes to a run across country, I'd expect my master to win every time. He has hunted here, as man and boy, for nearly 50 years. But they'll catch Merlyn before he starts to run, if I'm not mistaken.'

The steep hill to Jamaica Inn rose in front of them, white beneath the moon, and as the dark chimneys rose into view, Richards became silent, examining his guns. As they came near to the top of the hill, Richards turned, and whispered in her ear, 'Would it be best for you to wait here, in the carriage, by the side of the road, while I go forward to see if they are there?'

'I've waited long enough tonight, and gone half crazy with it,' said Mary. 'I'd rather meet my uncle face to face than stay behind here, seeing and hearing nothing. It's my aunt I'm thinking of. She's as harmless as a child, and I want to take care of her if I can. Give me a gun and let me go. I won't take any risks, I promise you.'

She went forward, then held her gun in front of her and looked round the corner of the stone wall into the yard. It was empty. The stable door was shut. The inn was as dark and silent as when she had left it nearly seven hours before; the windows and the door were barred. There were no wheel marks in the yard, and no preparations for escape. She crept across to the stable and laid her ear against the door. She waited a moment, and then she heard the horse move restlessly, she heard his feet on the stone floor.

Then they had not gone, and her uncle was still at Jamaica Inn!

Her heart sank, and she wondered if she should return to Richards and wait until the magistrate and his men arrived. Surely, if her uncle intended to leave, he would have gone before now? He might have changed his plans and decided to go on foot, but then Aunt Patience could never go with him.

Mary went round the corner of the house. She came to where a crack of light would show through the kitchen window shutter. There was no light. She laid her hand on the handle of the door. It turned, to her surprise, and the door opened. This easy entrance, completely unexpected, surprised her for the moment and she was afraid to enter. Supposing her uncle sat on his chair, waiting for her, his gun across his knee? She had her own gun, but it gave her no confidence.

Very slowly she put her face around the door. No sound came to her. Out of the corner of her eye she could see the ashes of the fire, but they were hardly red. She knew then that the kitchen had been empty for hours. She pushed the door open, and went inside. She lit the lamp and looked about her.

The door to the passage was wide open, and the silence became more frightening than before, strangely and terribly still. Something was not as it had been; some sound was missing that must account for the silence. Then Mary realized that she could not hear the clock. It had stopped. She stepped into the passage and listened again. She was right; the house was silent because the clock had stopped.

She turned the corner, and she saw that the clock, which always stood against the wall beside the door, had fallen forward on to its face. The glass was in pieces on the stone floor, and the wood had split. The clock had fallen across the narrow hall, and it was not until she came to the foot of the stairs that Mary saw what was beyond it.

The landlord of Jamaica Inn lay on his face among the broken glass.

The fallen clock had hidden him at first; he lay in the shadow, one arm thrown above his head and the other holding the door. There was blood on the stone floor; and blood between his shoulders, dark now and nearly dry, where the knife had entered him.

When he was attacked from behind, he must have stretched out his hands, and fallen, dragging at the clock; and when he fell on his face, the clock had crashed with him to the ground, and he had died there, trying to reach the door.

Chapter 14   The Pedlar Is Found

It was a long time before Mary moved away from the stairs. Something of her own strength had gone, leaving her powerless like the figure on the floor. It was the silence that frightened her most. Now that the clock was no longer going, her ears missed the sound of it. Her light shone on the walls, but it did not reach to the top of the stairs, where the darkness waited for her. She knew that she could never climb those stairs again, nor walk along that upper passage. Whatever lay above her must stay there.

She backed away down the hall along the passage, and when she came to the kitchen and saw the door still open, her self-control left her, and she ran blindly through the door to the cold air outside, where the familiar figure of Richards met her. He put out his hands to save her, and she seized him, feeling for comfort, cold now from the shock.

'He's dead,' she said; 'he's dead there on the floor. I saw him'; and, although she tried hard, she could not stop shaking. He led her to the side of the road, back to the carriage.

'Has your aunt gone?' he whispered.

Mary shook her head. 'I don't know. I didn't see. I had to come away.'

He saw by her face that her strength had gone. 'All right, then,' he said, 'all right. Sit quiet, then. No one shall hurt you. There now.' His rough voice helped her, and she sat close beside him.

'That was no sight for a girl to see; you should have let me go. I wish now you'd stayed back here in the carriage. That's terrible for you, to see him lying there, murdered.'

Talking helped her. 'The horse was still in the stable. I listened at the door and heard it moving about. They had never even finished their preparations for going. The kitchen door was not locked, and there were packages on the floor there, ready to load into the wagon. It must have happened several hours ago.'

'I don't know what the magistrate is doing,' said Richards. 'He should have been here before this. You should tell your story to him. There's been bad work here tonight.'

They fell silent, and both of them watched the road.

'Who could have killed the landlord?' said Richards confused. 'He can deal with most men, and should have been able to defend himself. There were plenty who might have done it, though. If ever a man was hated, he was.'

'There was the pedlar,' said Mary slowly. 'I'd forgotten about him. It must have been him, breaking out from the locked room.'

She seized on this idea, to escape from another; and she retold the story, eagerly now, of how the pedlar had come to the inn the night before. It seemed then that the crime was proved, and there could be no other explanation.

'He'll not run far before the magistrate catches him,' said Richards. 'No one can hide on these moors, unless he's a local man, and I've never heard of Harry the pedlar before. But then, they came from every hole and corner in Cornwall, Joss Merlyn's men. They were the lowest of the low from the whole area.'

He paused, and then: 'I'll go to the inn, if you would like me to, and see for myself whether he has left any tracks behind him. There might be something . . .'

Mary seized hold of his arm. 'I don't want to be alone again,' she said quickly. 'Think me a fool if you will, but I couldn't bear it. If you had been inside Jamaica Inn tonight you would understand . . . Something has happened to my aunt as well. I know that. I know she is dead. That's why I was afraid to go upstairs. She's lying there in the darkness, in the passage above. Whoever killed my uncle will have killed her too.'

The servant coughed. 'She may have run out on to the moor. She may have run for help along the road.'

'No,' whispered Mary, 'she would never have done that. She would be with him now, by his side. She's dead. I know she's dead. If I hadn't left her, this would never have happened.'

The man was silent. He could not help her. After all, she was a stranger to him, and what had happened was no concern of his.

Mary held up a warning hand. 'Listen,' she said. 'Can you hear something?'

They looked to the north. The distant sound of horses was unmistakable. 'It's them!' said Richards excitedly. 'It's the magistrate; he's coming at last.'

They waited. The noise drew near, and Richards in his relief ran out on to the road to greet them, shouting and waving his arms. The leader pulled up his horse, calling out in surprise at the sight of him. 'What are you doing here?' he shouted. It was Mr Bassat himself. He held up his hand to warn his followers behind.

'The landlord is dead, murdered!' cried his servant. 'I have a young relative of his here with me in the carriage. It was Mrs Bassat who sent me out here, sir.' He held the horse for his master, answering as well as he could the rapid questions put to him. 'If the man has been murdered, he deserved it, but I'd still rather have put him in chains myself. You cannot punish a dead man.'

The magistrate, whose mind worked slowly, began to realize what Mary was doing in the carriage. He had thought at first that she was his servant's prisoner. 'This is too difficult for me to understand,' he said. 'I believed you to be working with your uncle against the law. Why did you lie to me, when I came earlier in the month? You told me you knew nothing.'

'I lied because of my aunt,' said Mary. 'Whatever I said to you then was only for her, nor did I know as much then as I do now.'

'You did a brave thing in walking all that way to Altarnun to warn me; but all this trouble could have been avoided, and the terrible crime of that night could have been prevented if you had been open with me before. But we can talk about that later. I must ask you to wait in the yard.'

He led his men round the back, and before long the dark and silent house seemed to come to life. The windows were thrown open, and some of the men went upstairs and explored the rooms above. Someone called sharply from the house. After a time the magistrate himself came out into the yard and walked over to the carriage.

'I'm sorry,' he said. 'I have bad news for you. Perhaps you expected it.'

'Yes,' said Mary.

'I don't think she suffered at all. She was lying just inside the bedroom at the end of the passage. Killed with a knife, like your uncle. She could have known nothing. Believe me, I'm very sorry. I wish I could have kept this from you.' He stood by her awkwardly; and then, seeing that Mary was better left alone, he walked back across the yard to the inn. Mary sat without moving and prayed in her own way that Aunt Patience would understand what she had tried to do, and would forgive her and find peace now, wherever she might be.

Once again, there was excitement in the house – shouting and the sound of running feet. There was a crash of splitting wood and the shutters were torn away from the windows of the locked room, which no one, it seemed, had entered until now. Then round the corner of the yard they came, six or seven of them led by the magistrate, holding among them something that fought to escape. 'They've got him! It's the murderer!' shouted Richards. The prisoner looked up at her, his face and clothes dirty; it was Harry the pedlar.

'What do you know of this man?' the magistrate said to Mary. 'We found him in the locked room there, lying on the floor. He says he knows nothing of the crime.'

'He was one of the company,' said Mary slowly, 'and he came to the inn last night and quarrelled with my uncle. My uncle aimed a gun at him, and locked him up in the locked room, threatening him with death. He had every reason to kill my uncle, and no one could have done it except him. He is lying to you.'

'But the door was locked; it took three of us to break it down from the outside. This man had never been out of the room at all. Look at his clothes; look at his eyes, blinded still by our light! He's not your murderer.'

Mary knew then that what Mr Bassat had said was the truth. Harry the pedlar could not have done the murders.

'We'll have him in prison, in spite of that, and hang him too, if he deserves it, which I'll swear he does. But first he shall give us the names of his companions. One of them has killed the landlord, you may be sure of that, and we'll track him down if we have to set every dog in Cornwall on his heels.'

They dragged the pedlar away, swearing and begging them to let him go, turning his rat's eyes now and again on Mary, who sat above him in the carriage a few yards away.

She neither heard his curses nor saw his ugly narrow eyes. She remembered other eyes that had looked at her that morning, and another voice that had spoken calmly and coldly, saying of his brother: 'He shall die for this.' There was the sentence, thrown out carelessly on the way to Launceston fair: 'I have never killed a man – yet'; and there was the old woman in the market square: 'There's blood on your hands; you'll kill a man one day.' All the little things she wanted to forget rose up and shouted against Jem: his hatred of his brother, his cruelty, his bad Merlyn blood. He had gone to Jamaica Inn as he had promised, and his brother had died, as he had sworn. The whole truth was there in front of her in its ugliness. He was a thief, and like a thief in the night he had come and gone again. When morning came he would jump on a horse, and ride away out of Cornwall for ever, a murderer like his father before him.

In her imagination she heard the sound of his horse on the road, far away in the quiet night. But the sound she heard was not the dream thing of her imagination, but the real sound of a horse coming towards her. She turned her head and listened. The sound of a horse drew nearer still. She was not alone now as she listened. The men looked towards the road, and Richards went quickly to the inn to call the magistrate. The sound of the horseman was loud now as he came over the top of the hill, and when he came into view Mr Bassat came out of the inn.

'Stop!' he called. 'In the name of the King. I must ask your business on the road tonight.'

The horseman turned into the yard. When he took off his hat, his thick hair shone white under the moon, and the voice that spoke in answer was gentle and sweet.

'Mr Bassat of North Hill, I believe,' he said, and he leant forward, with a note in his hand. 'I have a message here from Mary Yellan of Jamaica Inn, who asks for my help in trouble; but I see by the company here that I came too late. You remember me, of course; we have met before – I am the Vicar of Altarnun.'

Chapter 15   The Truth Is Told

Mary sat alone in the living room in the vicar's house and looked into the fire. She had slept for a long time, and now felt rested, but the peace which she desired had not yet come to her. They had all been kind to her, and patient. The vicar had driven her himself in the carriage to Altarnun, and they arrived there as his church clock struck one. He called his housekeeper from her home near by, the same woman that Mary had spoken with in the afternoon. She lit a fire and warmed a rough woollen nightdress in front of it, while Mary took off her clothes, and when the bed was ready for her and the bedclothes turned back, Mary allowed herself to be led to it like a child.

She would have closed her eyes immediately but an arm came suddenly round her shoulders and a voice said in her ear: 'Drink this.' Francis Davey himself stood beside the bed, with a glass in his hand, his strange eyes looking into hers, pale and expressionless. 'You will sleep now,' he said, and she knew from the bitter taste that he had put some powder in the hot drink which he had made for her. The last thing she remembered was those still white eyes that told her to forget; and then she slept.

It was nearly four in the afternoon before she woke. When she was dressed, and had gone below to the living room, to find the fire burning and the curtains closed and the vicar out on some business, it seemed to her that responsibility for the murders was hers alone. Jem's face was always with her as she had seen it last, tired and lined in the grey light, and there had been a determination in his eyes then that she had tried not to see. He had played an unknown part from beginning to end, and she had shut her eyes to the truth. She was a woman, and for no good reason — in fact, against all reason — she loved him. He had kissed her, and she was tied to him for ever. She felt herself weakened in mind and body, she who had been strong before.

One word to the vicar when he returned, and a message to the magistrate, and Jem would die with a rope round his neck as his father had done, and she would return to Helford and her old life. But she knew that the word would never be given. Jem was safe from her, and he could ride away with a song on his lips, forgetful of her, and of his brother, and of God; while she dragged through the years, bitter and miserable, coming in the end to be known as a woman who had been kissed once in her life and could not forget it.

She heard the vicar's footsteps on the path outside, and rose hurriedly.

'Forgive me,' he said. 'You did not expect me so soon.' He took out his watch. 'You have had supper with me before, Mary Yellan, and you shall have supper with me again; but this time, if you do not mind, you shall prepare the table and bring the food from the kitchen. I have some writing to do; that is, if you have no objection.'

When the church clock said quarter to seven they sat down together at the table and he helped her to some cold meat.

'I understand from Richards, servant to Mr Bassat, that you suspected the pedlar of the murder, and said so to Mr Bassat himself. It is a pity for all of us that the locked room proves that he did not do it. He would have done very well as a man to hang, and saved a lot of trouble.' The vicar ate an excellent supper, but Mary was only playing with her food. He watched her. 'What has the pedlar done, that you hate him?'

'He attacked me once.'

'I thought so. You managed to fight him off?'

'I believe I hurt him. He didn't touch me again.'

'No. I don't suppose he did. When did this happen?'

'On Christmas Eve.'

'After I left you in the carriage?'

'Yes.'

'I'm beginning to understand. You didn't return, then, to the inn that night. You met the landlord and his friends on the road?'

'Yes.'

'And they took you with them to the shore to add to their sport?'

'Please, Mr Davey, do not ask me any more. I would rather not speak of that night ever again. There are some things that are best buried deep.'

'You shall not speak of it, Mary Yellan. I blame myself for having allowed you to continue your journey alone . . . Turning back to the pedlar, though, I feel it was very careless of the murderer not to have looked into the locked room. He would most certainly have made the whole affair more thorough.'

'You mean, he might have killed the pedlar too?'

'Exactly. If the murderer had known that he had attacked you, he would have had a strong enough reason to kill the pedlar twice over.'

Mary cut herself a piece of cake which she did not want, and forced it between her lips. But the hand that held the knife was shaking.

'I don't see,' she said, 'how I am involved in the matter.'

'You have too low an opinion of yourself.'

They continued to eat in silence, Mary with lowered head and eyes fixed on her plate. She knew that he was watching her to see the effect of his words. But at last she could wait no longer, and a question burst from her: 'So Mr Bassat and the rest of you have made little progress after all, and the murderer is still free?'

'The organization appears to have been far larger than was formerly supposed. In fact, the pedlar even suggested that the landlord of Jamaica Inn was their leader in name only, and that your uncle had orders from someone above him. That of course makes things look very different. What have you to say about the pedlar's idea?'

'It is possible, of course.'

'I believe that you once made the same suggestion to me?'

'I may have done. I forget.'

'If this is so, it would seem that the unknown leader and the murderer must be the same person. Don't you agree?'

'Well, yes, I suppose so.'

'That should make the search easier. We may forget most of the company, and look for someone with a brain and some character. Did you ever see such a person at Jamaica Inn?'

'No, never.'

'He must have moved about secretly, possibly in the silence of the night when you and your aunt were asleep. He would not have come by the road, because you would have heard the noise of his horse. So the man must know the moors. That is why Mr Bassat intends to question every local man within 10 miles. So you see the net will close round the murderer, and if he stays long he will be caught. We are all sure of that. Have you finished already? You have eaten very little.'

'I'm not hungry.'

'I'm sorry about that. Did I tell you that I saw a friend of yours today?'

'No, you didn't. I have no friends but yourself.'

'Thank you, Mary Yellan. That's a kind thing to say to me. But you're not being strictly truthful, you know. You have a friend; you told me so yourself.'

'I don't know who you mean, Mr Davey.'

'Come, now. Didn't the landlord's brother take you to Launceston fair?'

Under the table, Mary dug her fingernails into her flesh.

'The landlord's brother?' she repeated in order to delay her answer. 'I haven't seen him since then. I believed him to be away.'

'No, he has been in the area since Christmas. He told me so himself. As a matter of fact, it had come to his ears that I had given you shelter, and he came up to me with a message for you. "Tell her how sorry I am." That is what he said. I imagine that he meant that he was sorry about your aunt. It was just before I came away from North Hill this evening when the discussion had ended for the day.'

'Why was Jem Merlyn present at this discussion?'

'He had a right, I suppose, as brother of the dead man. He did not appear much moved by his death, but perhaps they were not close.'

'Did – did Mr Bassat and the gentleman question him?'

'There was a great deal of talk among them the whole day. Young Merlyn appears to have brains. His answers were very clever. He must have far better brains than his brother ever had. You told me he lived rather riskily, I remember. He steals horses, I believe.'

Mary agreed. Her fingers followed a pattern on the tablecloth.

'He seems to have done that when there was nothing better to do, but when a chance came for him to use his brains, he took it, and one cannot blame him, I suppose. No doubt he was well paid.'

The gentle voice wore away at her, and she knew that he had defeated her. She could no longer pretend that she did not care.

'What will they do to him, Mr Davey? What will they do to him?'

The pale, expressionless eyes looked back at her, and for the first time she saw a shadow pass across them and a momentary surprise.

'Do?' he said. 'Why should they do anything? I suppose he has made his peace with Mr Bassat and has nothing more to fear. They will hardly try to punish him for old crimes after the service he has done them.'

'I don't understand you. What service has he done?'

'Your mind works slowly tonight, Mary Yellan. Did you not

know that it was Jem Merlyn who informed against his brother?'

She looked at him stupidly, her brain refusing to work. She repeated the words after him like a child who learns a lesson. 'Jem Merlyn informed against his brother?'

The vicar pushed away his plate, and began to clear the table. 'Yes, certainly. It appears that it was Mr Bassat himself who took away your friend from Launceston that night, and carried him off to North Hill. "You've stolen my horse," he said, "and you're as big a criminal as your brother. I've the power to throw you into prison tomorrow, and you wouldn't set eyes on a horse for ten years or more. But you can go free if you bring me proof that your brother at Jamaica Inn is the man I believe him to be."

'Your young friend said "No! You must catch him yourself if you want him." But the magistrate told him about the latest, bloodiest wreck and suggested he changed his mind. I understand that your friend escaped from his chains, though, and ran away in the night; but he came back yesterday morning, when they did not expect to see him again, and went straight up to the magistrate and said, as calmly as you please. "Very well, Mr Bassat, you shall have your proof." And that is why I remarked to you just now that Jem Merlyn has a better brain than his brother had.'

Mary looked blindly before her into space, her whole mind split, as it were, by his information, the evidence she had so fearfully and so painfully built against the man she loved falling like a house of cards.

'Mr Davey,' she said slowly, 'I believe I am the biggest fool that ever came out of Cornwall.'

'I believe you are, Mary Yellan,' said the vicar.

After the gentle voice that she was used to, the sharpness of these words was a punishment in itself.

The anxiety and fear had gone from her at last.

'What else did Jem Merlyn say and do?' she asked.

The vicar looked at his watch. 'I wish I had time to tell you,' he said, 'but it is nearly eight already. The hours go by too fast for both of us. I think we have talked enough about Jem Merlyn for the present.'

'Tell me something – was he at North Hill when you left?'

'He was. In fact, it was his last remark that hurried me home.'

'What did he say to you?'

'He was not speaking to me. He told Mr Bassat he intended to ride over tonight to visit the blacksmith at Warleggan. It's a long way from North Hill, but I expect he can find his way in the dark.'

'What has it to do with you if he visits the blacksmith?'

'He will show him the nail he picked up in the grass down in the field below Jamaica Inn. The nail comes from a horse's shoe; the work was carelessly done, of course. The nail was a new one, and Jem Merlyn, being a stealer of horses, knows the work of every blacksmith on the moors. "Look here," he said to the magistrate. "I found it this morning in the field behind the inn. I'll ride to Warleggan with your permission, and throw this in Tom Jory's face as an example of bad work."'

'Well, and what then?'

'Yesterday was Sunday, was it not? And on Sunday no blacksmith works unless he has a special respect for his customer. Only one traveller passed Tom Jory's workshop yesterday, and begged for a new nail for his horse's shoe, and the time was, I suppose, somewhere near seven o'clock in the evening. After which, the traveller continued his journey – a journey which included a visit to Jamaica Inn.'

'How do you know this?' said Mary.

'Because the traveller was the Vicar of Altarnun,' he said.

Chapter 16   The Night on the Moors

A silence had fallen on the room. Although the fire burnt as steadily as ever, the air was cold as it had not been before. Each waited for the other to speak, and Mary heard Francis Davey swallow once. At last she looked into his face, and saw what she expected: the pale, steady eyes looking at her across the table, cold no longer, but burning in his white face like living things. She knew now what he wanted her to know, but still she said nothing, trying to gain time to think.

'There is no longer any need for us to pretend,' he said. 'You say to yourself, "What sort of man is this Vicar of Altarnun?" You say, "He is a strange product of nature, and his world is not my world." You are right, Mary Yellan. I live in the past – long ago in the beginning of time, when the rivers and the sea were one, and the old gods walked the hills.'

He rose from his chair and stood before the fire, a thin black figure with white hair and pale eyes, and his voice was gentle now, as she had known it first.

'If you studied history you would understand,' he said, 'but you are a woman, living in the nineteenth century, and because of this my language is strange to you. Yes, I am a strange product of nature and of time. I do not belong here, and I was born with a desire for revenge against our times and against the human race. Peace is very hard to find in the nineteenth century. The silence has gone, even on the hills. I hoped to find it in the church, but its teaching is false. We can talk of these things later, though, when we are no longer being hunted. One thing at least – we have nothing to carry and can travel light, as they travelled in the old days.'

Mary looked up at him, holding tightly to the sides of her chair.

'I don't understand you, Mr Davey.'

'You do; you understand me very well. You know by now that I killed the landlord of Jamaica Inn, and his wife too; nor would the pedlar have lived if I had known of his existence. You have put the story together in your own mind, while I talked to you just now. You know that it was I who directed every move made by your uncle, and that he was a leader in name alone. He was powerless without my orders, but the greater his fame among his companions the better he was pleased. We were successful, and he served me well; no other man knew our secret – that we were partners.

'You were the difficulty, Mary Yellan. When you came among us, I knew that the end was near. In any case we had played the game to its limit and the time had come to make an end. How you troubled me with your courage and your sense of justice, and how I admired you for them! Of course you had to hear me in the empty bedroom at the inn, and had to creep down to the kitchen and see the rope on the beam; that was the first piece of trouble that you caused.

'And then you had to go out on the moor after your uncle, who had an appointment with me on Roughtor, and, losing him in the darkness, meet myself and tell me your secrets. Well, I became your friend, did I not, and gave you good advice? Which, believe me, could not have been improved on by the magistrate himself. Your uncle knew nothing of our strange friendship. He caused his own death, by disobeying me. I knew something of your determination, and that time alone would quieten your suspicions. But your uncle had to drink himself crazy on the night before Christmas and, behaving like a fool, put the whole country in a fever. I knew then that when the rope was round his neck he would play his last card and name me as the leader. Therefore he had to die, Mary Yellan, and your aunt, who was his shadow; and, if you had been at Jamaica Inn last night when I passed by, you too – no, you would not have died.'

He leant down to her and, taking her two hands, he pulled her to her feet, so that she stood level with him, looking into his eyes.

'No,' he repeated, 'you would not have died. You would have come with me as you will come tonight.'

She looked back at him, watching his eyes. They told her nothing – they were clear and cold as they had been before – but his hold on her arms was firm.

'You are wrong,' she said. 'You would have killed me then as you will kill me now. I am not coming with you, Mr Davey.'

'You have proved yourself a dangerous enemy, and I prefer to have you by my side. In time, we will be able to return to our first friendship.'

'Any friendship we have shared was disgusting and dishonourable. You wear the clothes of a priest of God to hide you from suspicion. You talk to me of friendship–'

'Your refusal and anger please me more than anything, Mary Yellan,' he replied. 'There is a fire about you that the women of the old days possessed. Your company is not a thing to be thrown to one side. Are you ready? You understand me, the house is empty, and your cries would be heard by no one. I am stronger than you might suppose. Your uncle knew my strength! I don't want to hurt you, Mary Yellan, but I shall have to if you try to fight me. Come, where is that spirit of adventure that you have made your own? Where is your courage?'

She saw by the clock that he must already have used up his allowance of time. It was half past eight, and by now Jem would have spoken with the blacksmith at Warleggan. Twelve miles lay between them perhaps, but no more. She thought rapidly, weighing the chances of failure and success. If she went now with Francis Davey she could slow him down. The law would follow close behind him, and her presence would show them where he was in the end. If she refused to go, then there would be a knife in her heart, at best.

She smiled then, and looked into his eyes, having made her decision.

'I'll come with you, Mr Davey,' she said, 'but you will be sorry in the end.'

'I'll like you the better for it. I'll teach you to live, Mary Yellan, as men and women have not lived for 4,000 years or more.'

'You'll find me no companion on the road, Mr Davey.'

'Road? Who spoke of roads? We go by the moors and hills, and put our feet on stone and grass as the ancient men did before us.'

She went into the passage. She was filled with the wild spirit of adventure, and she had no fear of him, and no fear of the night. Nothing mattered now, because the man she loved was free and had no mark of blood on him. She could love him without shame; she knew that he would come to her again. She imagined she heard him ride along the road after them, and she heard his victorious cry.

She followed Francis Davey. The sight of horses was one for which she was not prepared.

'Do you not plan to take the carriage?' she said.

'No, Mary, we must travel light and free. You can ride — every woman born on a farm can ride — and I shall lead you.'

The night was dark, with a cold wind. The sky was filled with low cloud, and the moon was hidden. There would be no light on the way, and the horses would travel unseen. She climbed onto hers, wondering whether a shout and a wild cry for help would wake the sleeping village, but even as the thought passed through her mind she saw the flash of steel in his hand, and he smiled.

'That would be a fool's trick, Mary,' he said. 'They go to bed early in Altarnun, and by the time they were awake and rubbing their eyes I would be away over the moor and you — you would be lying on your face in the long wet grass with your youth and beauty spoilt. Come now!'

She said nothing. She had gone too far in her game of chance, and must play it to the finish. He climbed on the other horse, tied hers to it, and they set out on their strange journey.

They came to the edge of the moor and the rough track leading to the stream, and then headed across the stream and beyond to the great black heart of the moor, where there were no tracks and no paths. The tors rose up around them and hid the world behind, and the two horses were lost between the steep hills. Mary's hopes began to fail, as she looked over her shoulder at the black hills that rose behind her. There was an ancient mystery about these moors. Francis Davey knew their secrets, and he cut through the darkness like a blind man in his home.

'Where are we going?' she said, at last, and he turned to her, smiling beneath his wide black hat, and pointed to the north.

'The Atlantic has been my friend before. A ship shall carry us from Cornwall. You shall see Spain, Mary, and Africa, and learn something of the sun; you shall feel the sand under your feet, if you wish. I care little where we go; you shall make the choice. Why do you smile and shake your head?'

'I smile because everything you say is wild and impossible. You know as well as I do that I shall run from you at the first chance – at the first village perhaps. I came with you tonight because you would have killed me otherwise, but in daylight, within sight and sound of men and women, you will be as powerless as I am now.'

'I am prepared for the risk. You forget that the north coast of Cornwall is very unlike the south. This north coast is as lonely as the moors themselves, and you will see no man's face but mine until we come to the place that I plan to reach.'

'Supposing then that the sea is reached, and we are on your ship, with the coast behind us. Name any place you please – Africa, or Spain. Do you think that I would follow you there and not tell about you, a murderer of men?'

'You will have forgotten it by then, Mary Yellan.'

'Forgotten that you killed my mother's sister?'

'Yes, and more besides. Forgotten the moors, and Jamaica Inn and your own foolish feet that crossed my path. Forgotten your tears on the road from Launceston, and the young man who caused them . . . Oh, don't bite your lip and look angry – I can guess your thoughts. I know the dreams and fears of women better than you do yourself.'

They rode on in silence, and after a time it seemed to Mary that the darkness of the night became thicker and the air closer, nor could she see the hills around her as she had before. The horses picked their way delicately, and now and again stopped as though uncertain of their way. The ground was soft and dangerous, and though Mary could no longer see the land on either side, she knew by the feel of the soft ground that they were surrounded by marshes. This explained the horses' fear, and she looked at her companion to discover his feelings. He leant forward, looking into the darkness that every moment became thicker, and she saw by his thin, tightly-closed mouth that he was using all his powers to find their way, threatened suddenly with this new danger. Mary thought of these same marshes as she had seen them in the light of day – the long brown grass blowing in the wind, while beneath them the black water waited in silence. She knew how the people of the moors themselves could go wrong, so that he who walked with confidence one moment could sink the next, without warning. Francis Davey knew the moors, but even he might lose his way.

She heard her companion swallow, and the little trick sharpened her fear. He looked to the right and left. And then, in front of them, barring their further progress, there rolled out of the night a great bank of low cloud, a white wall that blocked out everything.

Francis Davey stopped the horses; they stood trembling, the steam from their sides rising and mixing with the cloud. Then he turned to Mary, his white face as expressionless as ever.

'The gods have gone against me after all,' he said. 'To continue now among the marshes would be worse than to return. We must wait for the daylight.'

She said nothing, her first hopes returning to her, but then she remembered that the weather would be an enemy to the hunters as well as to the hunted.

He urged the horses to the left, away from the marsh, until they reached firmer ground and loose stones, while the white cloud moved up with them step by step.

'There will be rest for you, after all, Mary Yellan,' he said, 'and a hole in the rocks for your shelter and stone for your bed. Tomorrow may bring the world to you again, but tonight you shall sleep on Roughtor.' The horses climbed slowly out of the cloud to the black hills beyond.

Later, Mary sat with her back against a large stone. The great tor's broken top towered above them while below them the clouds hung unchanged. Up here the air was pure and clean. There was a wind that whispered in the stones; its breath, sharp as a knife and cold, blew on the rocks.

The horses were restless; they stood against a rock for shelter, and turned now and again towards their master. He sat apart, a few yards away from his companion, and sometimes she felt his eyes on her. He was king here, alone in the silence, with the great rocks to guard him and the cloud below to hide him. She thought how far they were from normal life. Here on the tor the wind whispered of fear, bringing old memories of violence and hopelessness, and there was a wild, lost note that sounded in the stone high above Mary's head, on the very top of Roughtor, as if the gods themselves stood there with their great heads lifted to the sky. She imagined she could hear the whisper of a thousand voices and the marching of a thousand feet, and she could see the stones turning into men beside her. Their faces were inhuman, older than time, as rough as the stone; and they spoke in a language that she could not understand, and their hands and feet were curved like the feet of birds. They turned their stone eyes on her, and looked through her and beyond, paying no attention, and she knew that she was like a leaf in the wind, while they lived on, undying creatures of ancient times. They came towards her, shoulder to shoulder, neither seeing nor hearing her, but moving like blind things to destroy her . . .

She woke from this dream to reality, feeling the vicar's hand on her mouth. She would have struggled with him, but he held her fast, speaking coldly in her ear and telling her to be still. He forced her hands behind her back and tied them, using his own belt.

Then he took a cloth from the pocket of his coat and folded it, and put it in her mouth, tying it behind her head so that any sound was now impossible. When he had done this he helped her to her feet, and he led her a little way beyond the rocks to the slope of the hill. 'I have to do this, Mary, for both of us,' he said. 'When we set out last night I did not expect this cloud. Listen to this, and you will understand why I have tied you up, and why your silence may still save us.'

He pointed downwards to the white cloud below. 'Listen,' he said again.

The darkness had broken above their heads and morning had come. To the east a faint light came before the pale sun. The cloud was with them still, and hid the moors below like a white sheet. Then she listened, as he had told her, and far away, from beneath the cloud, there came a sound between a cry and a call. It was too faint at first to tell what it was; unlike a human voice, unlike the shouting of men. It came nearer, and Francis Davey turned to Mary.

'Do you know what it is?' he said.

She looked back at him, and shook her head. She had never

heard the sound before. 'I'd forgotten that Mr Bassat keeps hunting dogs in his stables. It's a pity for both of us that I didn't remember.'

She understood; and with sudden fear of that distant eager crying she looked up at her companion, and from him to the two horses standing as patiently as ever by the side of the rock.

'Yes,' he said, following her eyes, 'we must let them loose and drive them down to the moors below. They would only lead the dogs to us.'

She watched him, sick at heart, as he untied the horses and led them to the steep slope of the hill. Then he bent down to the ground, picked up stones in his hands, and rained blow after blow on their sides; they ran off in fear, kicking stones and earth as they went, and so disappeared into the white clouds below. The crying of the dogs came nearer now, deep and continuous, and Francis Davey ran to Mary, pulling off his long black coat and throwing his hat away on to the grass.

'Come,' he said. 'Friend or enemy, we are both in danger now.'

They climbed up the hill among the stones and rocks, he with his arm round her, because her tied hands made progress difficult; and they ran in and out of pools, struggled knee-deep in wet grass, climbing higher and higher to the top of Roughtor. Here, on the very top, the stone was strangely shaped, twisted into the form of a roof. Mary lay beneath this great stone, breathless and bleeding. He reached down to her, and though she shook her head and made signs that she could climb no further, he bent and dragged her to her feet again, cutting at the belt that tied her and tearing the cloth from her mouth.

'Save yourself then, if you can!' he shouted, his eyes burning in his pale face, his white hair blowing in the wind. She held on to a table of stone some 10 feet from the ground, while he climbed above her and beyond, his thin black figure hanging on the smooth surface of the rock. The crying of the dogs was unearthly, coming as it did from the sheet of cloud below, and the sound was increased by the cries and shouting of men, a confusion that filled the air with sound and was the more terrible because it was unseen. The high clouds moved across the sky, and the yellow sun swam into view between them. The cloud below her melted away, and the land that it had covered for so long looked up at the sky, pale and new-born. Mary looked down the sloping hillside; there were little dots of men standing knee-deep in the long grass, while the dogs ran in front of them like rats among the fallen rocks.

They followed the track fast, 50 men or more, shouting and pointing up to the great tables of rock, and as they came near, the sound of the dogs filled the cracks and the hollows. Somebody shouted again, and a man who knelt on the ground about 50 yards from Mary lifted his gun to his shoulder and fired. The shot hit the rock without touching her, and when he rose to his feet she saw that the man was Jem, and that he had not seen her.

The dogs were running in and out among the stones, and one of them jumped up at the rock beneath her. Then Jem fired once more; and, looking beyond her, Mary saw the tall black figure of Francis Davey standing out against the sky, on a wide, flat rock high above her head. He stood for a moment, his hair blowing in the wind; and then he threw his arms wide, as a bird throws his wings to fly, and fell – down from his high rock to the wet grass and the little scattered stones below.

Chapter 17   A New Life

It was a hard, bright day in early January. The holes in the road, which were generally thick with mud or water, were covered with thin ice, and the wheel tracks were white. The air was cold.

Mary walked alone on the moor, and wondered why it was

that Kilmar, to the left of her, no longer seemed threatening. The moors were still empty, and the hills were friendless, but the old sense of evil had left them and she could walk on them without fear. She was free now to go where she chose, and her thoughts turned to Helford and the green valleys of the south. She had a strange desire in her heart for home and the sight of warm, friendly faces. She remembered with pain every smell and sound that had belonged to her for so long. She was from the soil and would return to it again, rooted to the earth as her fathers before her had been. Helford had given birth to her, and when she died she would be part of it once more. Only among the woods and streams of her own Helford valley would she know peace again.

There was a cart coming towards her from Kilmar, across the white moor. It was the one moving thing on the silent plain. She watched it with suspicion, for there were no houses on this moor except Trewartha, and Trewartha, she knew, stood empty. She had not seen its owner since he had fired past her at Roughtor. 'He's an ungrateful devil, like the rest of his family,' the magistrate had said. 'If I hadn't helped him, he'd be in prison now, with a long stay in front of him to break his spirit. I admit he did well. He was the means of finding you, Mary, and that black-coated murderer, but he's never even thanked me for clearing his name in the business, and has taken himself to the world's end, for all I know. There's never been a Merlyn yet that came to any good, and he'll go the same way as the rest of them.'

The cart came nearer to the slope of the hill. The horse bent to pull its load, and she saw that it was struggling with a strange pile of pots and pans and furniture. Someone was setting out on a journey with his house on his back. Even then she did not realize the truth, and it was not until the cart was below her and the driver, walking by its side, looked up to her and waved that she recognized Jem.

'Are you better?' he called, from beside the cart. 'I heard that you were ill, and had been staying in bed.'

'You must have heard wrong,' said Mary. 'I've been around the house at North Hill. There's never been much the matter with me except a hatred for this area.'

'There was some talk that you were to settle there, and be a companion to Mrs Bassat. Well, you'll lead an easy enough life with them, I dare say.'

'No. I'm going back home to Helford.'

'What will you do there?'

'I shall try to start the farm again, or at least work my way to it, because I haven't the money yet. I've friends there who will help me.'

'Where will you live?'

'I would be welcome in any house in the village. We're good neighbours in the south, you know.'

'I've never had neighbours, so I cannot say, but I've always had the feeling that it would be like living in a box, to live in a village. You put your nose over your gate into another man's garden, and if his flowers are better than yours there's an argument; and you know that if you cook a rabbit for your supper he'll have the smell of it in his kitchen. That's no life for anyone! Here's my home, Mary, all the home I've ever had, here on the cart, and I'll take it with me and set it up wherever I want to. I've been a wanderer since I was a boy; never any ties, nor roots, nor wishes, for any length of time; and I dare say I'll die a wanderer too. It's the only life in the world for me.'

'There's no peace, Jem, in wandering, and no quiet. There'll come a time when you'll want your own piece of ground, and your four walls, and your roof, and somewhere to rest your poor, tired bones.'

'The whole country belongs to me, Mary, with the sky for a roof and the earth for a bed. You don't understand. You're a woman, and your home is everything to you. I've never lived like that, and never shall. I'll sleep on the hills one night, and in a city the next. I like to find my fortune here and there and everywhere, with strangers for company and passers-by for friends. Today I meet a man on the road, and travel with him for an hour or for a year, and tomorrow he is gone again. We speak a different language, you and I.'

'Which way will you go?'

'Somewhere east of the river. It doesn't matter to me. I'll never come west again – not until I'm old and grey, and have forgotten many things. I thought of going to the north. They're rich up there, and open to new ideas; there'll be a fortune there for a man who goes to find it. Perhaps I'll have money one day, and buy horses instead of stealing them.'

'It's an ugly black country in the north.'

'I don't worry about the colour of the soil. Moorland soil is black, isn't it? And so is the rain when it falls among your pigs down at Helford. What's the difference?'

'You talk just to argue with me, Jem – there's no sense in what you say.'

'How can I be sensible when you lean against my horse with your hair blowing in the wind? I know that in five or ten minutes' time I shall be over that hill without you. My face will be turned towards the river and you will be walking back to North Hill to drink tea with Mr Bassat.'

'Delay your journey, then, and come to North Hill too.'

'Don't be a fool, Mary. Can you see me drinking tea with the magistrate, and dancing his children on my knee? I don't belong to his class, and neither do you.'

'I know that. And I'm going back to Helford because of it. I want to smell the river again, and walk in my own country.'

'Go on, then; turn your back on me and start walking now. You'll come to a road that will take you to Helford.'

'You're very hard today, and cruel.'

111

'I'm hard with my horses when they won't do as I say, but that doesn't mean that I love them any the less.'

'You've never loved anything in your life,' said Mary.

'I haven't had much use for the word, that's why,' he told her. 'It's past midday already, and I ought to be on the road. If you were a man I'd ask you to come with me, and you'd jump on to the seat and put your hands in your pockets and ride beside me for as long as it pleased you.'

'I'd do that now if you'd take me south.'

'Yes, but I'm going north – and you're not a man, you're only a woman, as you'd learn if you came with me. I'm going now. Goodbye.'

He took her face in his hands and kissed it, and she saw that he was laughing. 'When you're an old woman down in Helford, you'll remember that, and it will have to last you to the end of your days. "He stole horses," you'll say to yourself, "and he didn't care for women; but if I had not been so proud I'd have been with him now."'

He climbed onto the cart and looked down at her, waving his whip. 'I'll do 50 miles before tonight,' he said, 'and sleep like a child at the end of it, in a tent by the side of the road. I'll light a fire, and cook some eggs for my supper. Will you think of me or not?'

But she did not listen; she stood with her face towards the south, twisting her hands and saying nothing. Beyond those hills the empty moors turned to green grass, and the green grass to valleys and to streams. The peace and quiet of Helford waited for her beside the running water.

'It's not pride,' she told him; 'you know it's not pride; there's a sickness in my heart for home and all the things I've lost.'

He said nothing, but whistled to the horse. 'Wait,' said Mary, 'wait, and hold him still, and give me your hand.'

He laid the whip to one side, and reached down to her, and

swung her up beside him on the driver's seat.

'What now?' he said. 'And where do you want me to take you? You have your back to Helford, do you know that?'

'Yes, I know,' she said.

'If you come with me it will be a hard life, and a wild one at times, Mary, with no staying anywhere, and little rest or comfort. You'll get a poor exchange for your farm and little hope of the peace you look for.'

'I'll take the risk, Jem.'

'Do you love me, Mary?'

'I believe so, Jem.'

'Better than Helford?'

'I can't ever answer that.'

'Why are you sitting here beside me, then?'

'Because I want to, because I must; because now and for ever this is where I want to be,' said Mary.

He laughed then, and took her hand, and whipped the horse; and she did not look back over her shoulder again, but set her face north towards the river.

ACTIVITIES

Chapters 1–5

Before you read

1 Read the Introduction and match the information in **1-5** with the characters in **a-e**.

    a Mary Yellan   1 a criminal
    b Aunt Patience   2 a man of the Church
    c Joss Merlyn   3 Joss's wife
    d Jem Merlyn   4 the manager of an inn
    e Francis Davey   5 a newcomer to Jamaica Inn

2 Check the meaning of these words in your dictionary. They are all in the story.

    coach creep inn landlord magistrate marsh misery
    moor pedlar shutter stable tor wagon

    a Which three words refer to jobs?
    b Which three words refer to geographical features?
    c Which two words refer to transport?
    d Which three words refer to buildings or parts of buildings?
    e Which word is another word for unhappiness?
    f Which word describes a way that a person can move?

3 Are these statements true or false?

    a A *stable* is a place where horses are kept.
    b A *tor* is on higher ground than a *marsh* is.
    c A *magistrate* is the owner of an *inn*.
    d *Wagons* carry animals and *coaches* carry people.
    e *Pedlars* work in shops.
    f People build farms and villages on the *moors*.
    g Tragedy brings *misery* to people.
    h Thieves often *creep* around.
    i *Shutters* are the doors on a *coach*.
    j A *landlord* works for the local government.

4 Explain:

   a why Mary is travelling to Jamaica Inn.

   b why the coach driver is surprised that Mary wants to go there.

   c how Mary feels about her aunt's appearance.

   d what Joss's great weakness is.

   e how Joss's father and brother died.

   f why the bar is crowded on particular evenings.

   g what makes Mary think that there has been a murder.

   h the similarities between Joss and his brother.

   i how Jem steals horses.

   j why Mary does not report her suspicions to an officer of the law.

5 Describe Jamaica Inn and the countryside around it.

6 Take the parts of Mary and Aunt Patience. Using your own words, act out the scene in which Mary tries to find out what really happens at Jamaica Inn.

Chapters 6–10

Before you read

7 Choose three adjectives which you feel best describe each of these people:

   a Mary.   b Joss.   c Patience.   d Jem.

8 Find the words in *italics* in your dictionary and answer the questions.

   a What colour skin and hair does an *albino* have?

   b In what professions do *agents* work?

   c What is the date of Christmas *Eve*?

   d What kind of building does a *vicar* usually work in?

   e How do *eyelashes* protect the eyes?

   f What kinds of people or things are usually carried in (**a**) *carts* and (**b**) *carriages*?

After you read

9 Who is speaking to whom, and what are they talking about?

   a 'Nothing at all. The landlord has made a fool of me again.'

   b 'You've done well today . . . and I'll not forget it.'

c 'You're not fit to walk another step; and what's more, I'm not going to let you.'

d 'You ought to be ashamed of yourself.'

e 'But when they reach the shore they're dead men . . . Dead men tell no stories.'

f 'Did you ever see such a beautiful horse in your life? He holds his head just like poor Beauty did.'

g 'Tonight we shall all ride together proudly, perhaps for the last time. And you shall come with us.'

10 'Aunt Patience was a murderer too. She had killed by her silence.' Explain what Mary means by this. Do you agree with her? Why/why not?

11 Take the parts of Mary and the landlord. Using your own words, act out their argument after Mary's return from Launceston.

12 Describe the shipwreck that Mary witnesses.

Chapters 11–14

Before you read

13 Who does Mary feel that she can trust? Who can she not trust? Is there evidence to support her views?

14 What do you think will happen now to:

  a Joss Merlyn?   **b** Harry the pedlar?   **c** Aunt Patience?

15 What is this word in your language?

relief

Think of a situation when you were at first worried or frightened, but later you felt *relief*. Write about it.

After you read:

16 Who . . .

  a are Joss's enemies?

  b locks the pedlar in a room?

  c climbs up to Mary's window?

  d is the nearest magistrate to Altarnun?

  e takes Mary back to Jamaica Inn?

  f finds Joss Merlyn's body?

  g could not have killed Joss and Aunt Patience?

17 Answer the questions.

    a Why is Joss in no hurry to run from Jamaica Inn?

    b Why does the pedlar come to the inn?

    c Why does Mary leave the inn?

    d What brings the magistrate to the inn?

    e What brings the vicar there?

18 Imagine that you are Mary. The magistrate has just arrived at the inn and found the two bodies. Tell him where you have been and what you have been doing today, until the time when you found your uncle's body.

Chapters 15–17

Before you read

19 Who do you think killed Joss Merlyn and Aunt Patience? Give reasons for your opinion.

20 How do you think the story will end?

21 Describe the work of a blacksmith. Use a dictionary to help you.

After you read

22 Explain:

    a why Mary does not tell anyone her suspicions about Jem.

    b how Mary discovers that Jem is not the murderer.

    c how Mary discovers who the murderer is.

    d why Joss was murdered.

    e why Mary agrees to go with Francis Davey.

    f how Francis Davey plans to escape the law.

    g what Francis Davey does with his horses on the moor.

    h how Francis Davey dies.

23 Discuss why Mary goes with Jem in the end. Do you think she is making the right decision?

Writing

24 Compare the characters of Mary Yellan and Jem Merlyn. In what ways are they similar? In what ways are they different?

25 Describe the relationship between Joss and his wife. Basing your views on the story and on your own experience, how believable is it?

26 Explain why Mary trusts Francis Davey for so long, and how she discovers her mistake.

27 What part does the countryside play in the story?

28 Imagine that you are Mary. Write an account for the magistrate of the crimes that you witnessed on Christmas Eve.

29 Write a letter from Mary Yellan to a friend in Helford. Explain what has happened to your aunt and uncle and why you are not returning.